A FUGITIVE FROM LOVE

Salena Cardenham knew something was desperately wrong the moment she saw her father waiting for her at the Monte Carlo railway station.

"I think you have something to say to me, Papa," Salena said timidly.

"I have a great deal to say to you," Lord Cardenham replied, "but first let me explain where we are staying. Quite frankly, Salena, I am forced to rely on the generosity of my friends."

"Does that mean you are hard-up, Papa?"

"Not hard-up, broke! I have not a penny to my name."

"What can we do, Papa?"

"I will talk to you about that later," Lord Cardenham replied evasively. "In the meantime make yourself pleasant to our Russian host. You and I need a great deal from him, Salena. Unless he is willing to provide you with some new gowns, you'll wear what you have or go naked!"

"Papa!" It was a cry of dismay . . .

BARBARA CARTLAND

Bantam Books by Barbara Cartland
Ask your bookseller for the books you have missed

Barbara Cartland's Library of Love

Barbara Cartland
A Fugitive from Love

A FUGITIVE FROM LOVE
A Bantam Book / January 1978

ISBN 0-553-11649-5

Published simultaneously in the United States and Canada

Bantam Books are published by Bantam Books, Inc. Its trade-
mark, consisting of the words "Bantam Books" and the por-
trayal of a bantam, is registered in the United States Patent
Office and in other countries. Marca Registrada. Bantam
Books, Inc., 666 Fifth Avenue, New York, New York 10019.

PRINTED IN THE UNITED STATES OF AMERICA

Author's Note

Tangier at the beginning of the century was very different from the attractive place it is now—the streets were filthy, noisy, and crowded with camels, donkeys, beggars, and lepers.

The prison which was usually filled with criminals, brigands, and murderers provided no food and the prisoners had to rely on the charity of their friends. This resulted in most inmates being in a state of semi-starvation.

Moslem girls were married at the age of ten or twelve. The policy of the Government was oppression, bribery, injustice, and plunder.

Nevertheless, due to the marvellous, healthy climate, more and more English people as well as some Americans built Villas in the vicinity of Tangier.

Chapter One

1903

The train drew into Monte Carlo station, and Salena, stepping onto the platform, looked round her wide-eyed.

It appeared quite ordinary and was neither as exotic nor as menacing as she had been led to expect.

When the Mother Superior had learnt that she was to join her father at Monte Carlo she had been undisguisedly shocked.

She had in fact been so disapproving that Salena had been rather surprised, knowing that as a rule the Mother Superior was both tolerant and broad-minded.

The school, which was incorporated in a Convent, to which she had been sent two years ago, was not exclusively Catholic.

They admitted girls of all religions, but Salena was well aware that it was due to her step-grandmother's influence that she had been able to obtain a place.

"The Convent of St. Marie is extremely exclusive and will only take a limited number of pupils," the Dowager Lady Cardenham had told Salena, "but I believe the education is of a very high standard, and what is more important is that you should speak foreign languages."

She paused to say positively:

"If there is one thing that is essential for any girl today in the Social World, it is that she should be fluent in French and if possible also in Italian and German."

Salena had the idea that her step-grandmother had also chosen a Convent for her because she disapproved of the way her father was behaving after her mother's death.

It was no secret that the Dowager Lady Cardenham did not get on with her stepson and that it was only a sense of duty rather than affection which made her assume the responsibility of Salena's education.

"It is the only thing she does pay for," her father had said bitterly, "so do not pull your punches when it comes to having expensive books and extra classes —if there are such things."

There had been quite a number of the latter and Salena had felt embarrassed in knowing that at the end of the term her step-grandmother would receive a very large bill.

The Dowager Lady Cardenham could well afford it because she was a very rich woman, which made it all the more unfortunate that she should have died six months ago, before Salena was to make her début.

The other girls at the school talked incessantly about what they would do once they were grown up, the Balls that would be given for them, the social gaieties in which they would be included.

In consequence Salena had looked forward to the day when she would make her curtsey at Buckingham Palace and become one of the débutantes in what was always described as "a brilliant London scene."

She was fortunate in that the Dowager Lady Cardenham had paid her school fees a year ahead, but Salena had wondered apprehensively what she would do when the term came to an end and there was no provision made for her in the holidays.

She had never gone home to England from France after her mother's death.

Instead, the Mother Superior had arranged that with several other pupils whose parents were overseas, Salena should go with two of the nuns to a farm in the country and spend a few weeks in quiet if somewhat primitive surroundings.

Salena had loved every moment of it, but this last year she had found it sometimes frustrating to have so little to relate to her friends when she returned to school.

Nevertheless, she had been happy and it had come like a bomb-shell when first she learnt of her step-grandmother's death, and then received a letter from her father, telling her she was not to join him in London as she had expected but in Monte Carlo.

Monte Carlo!

The very name was synonymous with all that was raffish and wicked, despite the fact that the newspapers reported that all the Crowned Heads of Europe were gathered there at some time or another, including King Edward and his beautiful Danish-born wife, Queen Alexandra.

But the nuns regarded it as the nearest thing to hell on earth, and Salena half-expected to find the porters looking like devils and the engine of the train itself changed into a fire-breathing dragon.

Instead of which, as she stood looking round her, a smart footman came hurrying towards her to raise his tall, cockaded hat politely.

"*M'mselle* Cardenham?"

"*Oui, je suis Mademoiselle* Cardenham," Salena replied.

"*Monsieur* M'Lord is waiting for you in the carriage, *M'mselle*."

Salena turned eagerly to hurry from the station while the footman waited to collect her trunks.

Outside, in an open Victoria, leaning back and smoking a cigar, was her father.

"Papa!"

She gave a cry of delight and ran towards him, climbing into the carriage to sit beside him and lift her face to his.

She thought he looked at her scrutinisingly before he kissed her. Then he said in his usual jovial, good-humoured fashion:

"How are you, my poppet? I expected to say you have grown, but you are still the little midget you used to be."

"Actually, I am four inches taller than when you saw me last," Salena answered.

Lord Cardenham threw his cigar out of the side of the carriage, and putting both his hands on Salena's shoulders held her away from him.

"Let me look at you," he said. "Yes—I was right!"

"Right about what, Papa?"

"I had a bet with myself that you would grow into a beauty."

Salena blushed.

"I was hoping, Papa ... that you would think I was ... pretty."

"You are more than pretty," Lord Cardenham replied. "In fact you are beautiful, as beautiful as your mother was, but in a different way."

"I would love to look like Mama."

"I like to think you have a bit of me in you," Lord Cardenham said heartily. "Is the luggage coming?"

His last remark was made to the footman who had met Salena on the platform and was now standing beside the carriage.

"A porter is just bringing it, *Monsieur*."

"Is there much of it?"

"No, *Monsieur*."

"Then we will take it with us," Lord Cardenham said.

"Yes, *Monsieur*."

The porter appeared, carrying Salena's trunk

A *Fugitive from Love*

without any difficulty and a small valise which contained little except books.

"Is that all you possess?" Lord Cardenham enquired.

"I am afraid I have very few clothes, Papa. I have grown out of the gowns I wore before I went into mourning for Step-Grandmama, and there seemed to be no point in buying new ones, when I felt they would be no use once I had left school."

"No, of course not," Lord Cardenham replied.

He pulled an expensive, gold-cornered leather cigar-case from his pocket and opened it slowly in a manner which made Salena think that he was considering what he would say rather than concentrating on choosing a fresh cigar.

The luggage was by this time stowed away at the back of the Victoria and the footman climbed up on the box of the carriage as it moved off.

"I think you have something to say to me, Papa," Salena remarked quietly.

"I have a great deal to say to you, my dear," her father replied, "but first let me explain where we are staying."

"Are we staying with friends?" Salena asked, a note of disappointment in her voice. "I do so hope to be alone with you, Papa."

"That is what I would like myself," her father answered, "but quite frankly I have to rely on the generosity of my friends."

"Does that mean you are hard-up, Papa?"

"Not hard-up, Salena. Broke! I have not a penny to my name!"

"Oh no!"

It was a cry of distress, for Salena knew of old how hopeless her father always was about money, and how ever since she could remember she and her mother had had to skimp and save to make ends meet.

"I suppose," she said tentatively, "Step-Grandmama did not leave you anything in her will?"

5

"Leave me anything?" Lord Cardenham ejaculated. "She would rather leave it to the Devil himself! But what did surprise me was that she excluded you from her list of beneficiaries."

Salena did not speak and he went on:

"I know the reason. She loathed me and she thought that if you had any money I would spend it. It was in just the same way, blast him, that your mother's father behaved."

He paused; then buffing angrily at his cigar, he said:

"That means, my poppet, that you and I are down on our uppers. We have to think what we shall do about it and think fast."

Salena made a helpless little gesture with her hand.

"What can we do, Papa?"

"I have been turning several things over in my mind," Lord Cardenham said evasively, "but I will talk to you about that later. In the meantime, make yourself pleasant to our host."

"You have not yet told me who he is, Papa."

"His name is Prince Serge Petrovsky," her father replied.

"A Russian!" Salena exclaimed.

"Yes, a Russian, and a damned wealthy one at that! Monte Carlo is full of them, all as rich as Croesus, and, I am glad to say, generous with their money."

"But the Prince is your friend," Salena said. "I hope he does not mind including me as a guest."

"I explained to him frankly that I had nowhere to take you," Lord Cardenham answered, "and immediately he said you must come to the Villa. That was what I expected, but you and I need a great deal more from him than that."

Salena turned her face to look at her father in astonishment.

"More . . . Papa?"

"Even the most beautiful woman needs a frame."

6

"Papa, you are not suggesting . . ."

"I am not suggesting, I am telling you," her father said positively, "that unless the Prince is prepared to provide you with some new gowns you will wear what you have with you or go naked!"

"B-but . . . Papa . . . !"

It was a cry of dismay, and as if he felt embarrassed by it Lord Cardenham said almost roughly:

"Now listen to me, Salena, and listen carefully. When I say I am broke, I mean it. I am also in debt. So, to put it bluntly, you and I have to live by our wits."

"You are so clever and amusing, Papa, I am sure people are only too willing to offer you their hospitality, but it is a very different thing where I am concerned! To expect the Prince to pay for my clothes as well seems to me horrifying!"

"There is no alternative," Lord Cardenham said heavily.

"Are you . . . sure, Papa?"

"Do not suppose I have not thought of everything! But even living with other people is expensive one way or another: recently I have had bad luck with the cards and have even had to borrow money with which to tip the servants."

There was a note in her father's voice which told Salena exactly how much he was upset by this state of affairs, and although she thought that in the circumstances it was very risky to gamble, she was too wise to say so.

Instead, for the first time since they had left the station she took her eyes from her father's face and looked to where they were going.

They had moved out of the town and were now on a road with the sea on one side and high cliffs soaring above them on the other.

There was purple bougainvillaea climbing over bare rocks, a profusion of pink geraniums, and trees of golden mimosa which seemed to Salena to hold the sunshine.

"It is lovely! Oh, Papa, it is lovely!"

She looked out to sea and exclaimed:

"What a wonderful yacht! Do look at it, Papa."

A white steam yacht with the masts silhouetted against the sky was moving over the azure-blue water, leaving a silver wake.

With the white ensign flying from the stern, it had such a fairy-like quality that it was hard to guess why Lord Cardenham frowned as he remarked:

"That is the *Aphrodite*. It belongs to the Duke of Templecombe, curse him!"

"Why do you curse him, Papa?"

"Pure jealousy, my poppet—Templecombe is, next to Royalty, one of the most important men in England. He has houses, horses, and the best shoots! All the things I want and cannot have!"

"Poor Papa!"

"Not exactly," Lord Cardenham said. "I have one thing he doesn't possess."

"What is that?" Salena asked.

"A very lovely and sweet daughter!"

Salena gave a little laugh of happiness and laid her cheek against her father's shoulder.

"I am so very, very happy to be with you," she said softly.

"You will like the Prince's Villa," her father said. "It is very magnificent, although he did not build it himself. He bought it from some poor devil who lost everything at the tables and shot himself rather than face penury."

Salena gave a little shiver.

It was the sort of story she had heard before about Monte Carlo.

It flashed through her mind that she would hate to live in a house whose previous owner had deliberately taken his own life.

"It is a way out, which I have even considered myself," her father said heavily.

"Oh no, Papa! You must not say such . . . things!"

8

Salena cried. "It is . . . wrong. It is . . . wicked! Life is very . . . precious and is a gift from . . . God."

"It is a pity that God is not more generous in other ways," Lord Cardenham retorted.

Then he looked at Salena and said slowly:

"Yet I think perhaps He has been. He has certainly given me a very beautiful daughter."

Salena moved a little nearer to him and slipped her hand into his.

"It is so wonderful for me to hear you say that, Papa. The other girls at School used to laugh at me and say I looked such a baby that no-one would ever believe I was grown up."

"You certainly look very young," Lord Cardenham said.

Once again he inspected his daughter, and with a surprisingly poetical fancy he thought she looked like a flower.

Her small face with its pointed chin was dominated completely by her huge eyes. They should have been blue to complement the fairness of her hair, but instead they were grey with faint touches of green in some lights.

Set far apart, they held the trusting innocence of a child who has seen nothing of the world.

For the first time since he had thought of his daughter joining him, Lord Cardenham wondered if he was committing a sin against nature in bringing someone so transparently inexperienced to Monte Carlo.

Then he told himself there was no alternative, and perhaps the fact that she was so innocent would prevent her from understanding much that was said or happened.

Aloud he remarked:

"You will find a mixed collection of people staying with us at the Villa, but they all have one thing in common—they live to gamble."

"It is so beautiful," Salena said, looking out to sea. "There must be other things to do?"

9

"You will learn that they are not of importance," her father replied dryly.

"They will be important to me," Salena said, "because one thing is very obvious, Papa—I cannot afford to risk even one centime in case I lose it!"

"That is an indisputable fact," Lord Cardenham smiled.

The horses were turning off the road.

"Here we are," he said. "And let me tell you, I think this is one of the most attractive Villas in the whole of the Côte d'Azur."

They slowly descended a twisting drive of pine trees and walls covered with climbing geraniums.

Many feet below the road on which they had travelled, a Villa had been built on a small promontory jutting out into the sea.

Gleaming white in the sunshine, it was very impressive, and as they walked into the cool hall Salena felt she was stepping into fairy-land.

It was certainly very different from the high, narrow house off Eaton Square where she had lived when her mother was alive and which had always seemed to be too small for them.

Here was space and luxury, while the mirrors on the walls reflected the sunshine outside the windows, so that everything seemed dazzling.

Her father walked ahead of her through a long, exquisitely decorated Salon and out onto a terrace where there were blue awnings to protect the occupants from the sun.

There were only two people, sitting in low comfortable chairs. One of them was a lady, who struck Salena as being outstandingly beautiful; the other was a man, who rose to his feet to walk towards them.

"Well, here you are, Bertie," he said to Lord Cardenham. "I thought the train must be late."

"It was, but it arrived," Lord Cardenham replied. "Your Highness, may I present my daughter, Salena?"

Salena curtseyed and looked at the Prince with interest.

He was a man of about forty, who might, she thought, when he was young, have been good-looking. Now he was heavy, both in his features and in his body.

He had dark, rather protruding eyes, which inspected her in a manner which made her feel embarrassed.

His hair, streaked with grey at the temples, was brushed back from a square forehead and he had the look of a man who has lived too well for too long.

"I welcome you, Salena," he said in English, with a distinct accent. "As I expect your father has told you, I am delighted that you should be my guest."

"It is very kind of Your Highness," Salena murmured.

Her father was kissing the hand of the lady lounging back in the chair under the blue awning.

"*Madame* Versonne, I want you to meet my little Salena," Lord Cardenham said.

"But of course—I am delighted!" the Frenchwoman answered.

She did not, however, seem very delighted, and Salena felt that she looked her up and down disparagingly.

Salena curtseyed and waited to be told what she should do next.

Madame Versonne rose from her chair.

"Now that you have arrived," she said to Lord Cardenham, "I am going to rest. It is too hot for me here, but I was keeping Serge amused, at least I hope so."

She looked at the Prince provocatively and he responded with the compliment she obviously expected.

Then with her silken skirts moving sensuously and leaving behind an exotic fragrance on the air, *Madame* Versonne walked along the terrace to enter the Salon through the open window.

"Please sit down," the Prince said. "I am sure, Bertie, you need a drink after having to wait for your daughter's train in this unprecedented heat. I have never known it to be so hot in April."

Salena wanted to say that she thought it was delightful, but she was occupied in looking round her without appearing to be too inquisitive.

There was a long flight of white marble steps leading down from the terrace to the garden below and she realised that the Villa was on three different levels.

The garden which had been built on the promontory of rock which stuck out into the sea was only a little above sea-level.

There was a stone fountain playing in the centre of it, and there were large shady trees round a green lawn and flower-beds filled with exotic flowers, of which she could recognise only a few.

Beyond the garden, through the trees, she could see the sweep of the coast towards Monte Carlo, and on the other side, she thought, if she remembered rightly, towards the cliffs of Eze.

'How wonderful to be here,' she thought, 'and it is even more beautiful than I expected.'

The sea was vividly blue except for where towards the horizon it merged into an emerald green.

She had often heard the girls talk about the Côte d'Azur, but they had always stayed with their friends at Nice or Cannes.

Although they had talked with bated breath of Monte Carlo, none of them had ever visited the Principality.

'But I am here!' Salena thought to herself.

She wished for a moment that she could go back to school next term so that she would have more adventures to relate than any of the others.

"What are you thinking?" a deep voice asked, and she turned to the Prince with her eyes alight.

"It is so lovely!" she said. "I have read about the South of France and even studied some of its history, but I did not know it would be so enchanting."

The Prince smiled.

"It is what I felt myself when I first came here," he said. "But my country also is very beautiful."

"So I have always heard," Salena said.

She had also heard of the cruelties perpetrated in Russia and the suffering of the great majority of the population, but she did not think that was the sort of remark she should make.

She thought instead she should ask the Prince about the Russian Court and the magnificence of the Palaces in St. Petersburg.

But before she could formulate her question, her father, who was sitting on the other side of the Prince, said surprisingly:

"Take off that unattractive hat, Salena. I want His Highness to see your hair."

Salena looked at him in surprise, but because she was used to obeying orders she immediately took off her hat, feeling a little anxious that her hair might be untidy.

She had arranged it very simply in a knot at the back of her head, but released from the confines of the hat it rose above her oval forehead in a natural wave which held the sunshine.

"There is no-one more experienced than you, Serge," her father said, "when it comes to the female sex. So tell me, how should Salena dress and in what colours?"

"There is only one person in Monte Carlo who could do her justice," the Prince replied, "and that is Yvette. She is an artist in her own way and never makes the mistake of ruining a woman's personality by over-ostentatiousness, as so many other dressmakers do."

"Go on, Serge, I am listening," Lord Cardenham said. "I suspect that you too are an artist in your own way, or else it has something to do with the Russian temperament."

"The clothes of a beautiful woman must always be part of herself and her character," the Prince

13

said, "and never—remember this, Bertie—never must she become a 'clothes-horse.'"

"I will remember it," Lord Cardenham said, "but as far as I am concerned I can no more pay Yvette's prices than walk on the sea!"

He spoke without any trace of self-consciousness, but Salena felt the colour rising in her cheeks.

She was well aware why her father was drawing attention to her and she wished that she could run away and hide rather than hear him leading the conversation in a quite obvious manner round to what he required.

She was aware that the Prince too understood what her father intended, and with only a faint note of cynicism in his voice he replied:

"In my opinion, for anyone as lovely as your daughter, Bertie, only the best is good enough!"

"You mean that?" Lord Cardenham asked without any prevarication.

"Of course," the Prince answered. "Send a groom into Monte Carlo and tell Yvette to call as soon as possible. I imagine she knows her way here blindfolded."

"I am very grateful," Lord Cardenham said, "and I know Salena is grateful too. You must thank the Prince, my dear, for such a generous gift."

"Thank you ... thank you very ... much," Salena said obediently.

At the same time, she felt so embarrassed that she could not meet the Prince's eyes and a blush still burned in her cheeks.

It was degrading, she thought, that her father should have to ask openly for someone to pay for her clothes.

The Prince of course could well afford it, but she knew it would have shocked her mother and certainly horrified the Mother Superior.

There was a diversion when the servants arrived with a silver ice-bucket in which reposed a bottle of champagne.

A Fugitive from Love

Three glasses were laid on the table, but when they would have filled Salena's glass she put out her hand.

"No, thank you."

"You do not like champagne?" the Prince asked.

"I have not drunk it often," Salena answered, "only at Christmas and on Papa's birthday."

"You would prefer some lemonade?"

"Yes, please."

The Prince gave the order to the servants, then he said reflectively:

"You are to be envied, Salena, in that you are starting out in life and everything is new and interesting. I wonder how we would feel, Bertie, if we went back to when we were eighteen?"

"It is a long time ago," Lord Cardenham said. "But I remember being wildly excited when I won a point-to-point."

"I recall most vividly a love-affair at that age," the Prince said reflectively, "by no means my first, but I was infatuated to the point of madness. I saw the same ballet night after night and still found it entertaining."

Both men laughed and Salena thought that in the years to come when she looked back she would always remember her first glimpse of the South of France, the white yacht riding the blue of the Mediterranean.

When she had drunk her lemonade the Prince suggested she might like to see her bed-room.

"Yvette will be here soon," he said, "then we must choose the gown that you will need tonight and others that you can wear until she has time to provide you with everything that is necessary."

"I am sure I shall not...need too...much," Salena said quickly because she felt shy.

As she spoke she saw her father frown and knew he intended to take everything he could from the Prince.

Again she felt ashamed, and when she went up

15

to her bed-room to find that her clothes had been un-packed, she looked at the picture of her mother, which now stood on a dressing-table, and wondered what she would have thought.

It was only a sketch done by an amateur artist, because Lady Cardenham had never had the chance of being professionally painted, but the artist had caught the likeness and now Salena felt that her mother looked at her reproachfully.

"How can I help it?" she asked. "It is wrong of Papa, but I can hardly stay here with him in this grand Villa unless I have something respectable to wear."

Respectable was certainly not the right word to describe the gowns that Yvette brought with her from Monte Carlo.

She had not arrived as quickly as the Prince had anticipated, and because Salena had the idea that her father expected her to wait upstairs, she had lain on her bed to look through the window at the view outside.

It aroused her imagination, and she had been so deep in her thoughts that she had not realised the passing of time and felt when there was a knock on the door as if it brought her back to earth with a jerk.

The dressmaker was there with a vast number of cases and an assistant to unpack them.

Madame Yvette was a dark, vivacious French-woman, ugly but extremely *chic*.

"I have seen *Monsieur* your father," she informed Salena, "and His Highness, and they have told me that I am to dress you, *Mademoiselle,* in my special creations, then send you down to the Salon, where they are waiting to inspect them."

"That will . . . make me feel . . . very shy," Salena replied.

"You will not need to be shy when I have fin-ished dressing you, *Mademoiselle,*" *Madame* Yvette said. "But oo-la-la! How any lady can bear to be garbed as you are now is beyond my comprehension!"

Salena explained that she had just come from school and *Madame* accepted the explanation, but threw the plain, badly cut dress in which she had travelled to the floor in disgust.

When finally Salena was dressed in an evening-gown she looked at herself in the long mirror and thought she saw a stranger.

Madame Yvette had in fact started from the very beginning, by producing a close-fitting corset which was laced so as to reveal the tininess of Salena's waist.

"It is too tight, *Madame!*" Salena exclaimed, but the Frenchwoman paid no heed.

"Your figure is exquisite, *Mademoiselle!* It would be a sin to hide it!"

"But I find it hard to breathe."

"That is because you have allowed your body to become slack. That is wrong, very wrong. The body should always be contained and controlled."

A gown of white tulle, which revealed not only Salena's tiny waist but also the curves of her breasts and the whiteness of her skin, seemed very daring.

Yet at the same time there was an ethereal look about it which accentuated Salena's youth and her flower-like face.

Madame Yvette surveyed her critically.

"*C'est bien,*" she said. "It needs a little jewellery perhaps, but ..."

"No, no! Please do not ... mention such a thing," Salena interrupted.

She had an idea that her father would not hesitate to demand that from the Prince as well as everything else if he thought it necessary.

"Go to the Salon and show yourself," *Madame* Yvette said, "and afterwards I will find you a gown to wear tomorrow."

Salena did as she was told, but, at the same time, when she entered the Salon she felt very shy.

Her father and the Prince were sitting smoking and drinking on a sofa.

The sunblinds made the room cool and took away the brilliance of the light outside.

But Salena felt it was very revealing as she stood just inside the door, her eyes very wide in her small face, her fair hair seeming still to hold the sunlight.

"Let me look at you," the Prince said insistently.

"You are right, Serge," Lord Cardenham exclaimed, "that woman is a genius! I could not imagine a more appropriate gown to suit a young girl."

Salena moved slowly towards them.

She knew it was stupid but she wished that the gown was not so tight or so revealing.

She felt almost as if the Prince's dark eyes were staring at her naked, and she longed to be wearing the shapeless, rather ugly gown in which she had arrived.

"You look very beautiful!" the Prince remarked, "and doubtless a great number of other men will tell you so before the evening is over."

"I . . . hope not," Salena said quickly.

The Prince raised his eye-brows and she explained hesitatingly:

"I . . . I feel . . . shy if people . . . notice me . . . but perhaps you are . . . just being . . . kind."

"Of course I am being kind," the Prince answered, "and I am ready to be very much kinder."

"Y-yes . . . I know . . . and I am very . . . grateful," Salena said stumbling over her words, feeling as if she was not expressing herself at all coherently.

She had a longing to be back at School where she did not say the wrong thing and where no-one looked at her in a manner which made her feel uncomfortable.

When she felt she could bear it no longer she turned towards the door.

"*Madame* has another gown for me to show you," she said and ran from the Salon.

* * *

Some hours later when Salena was putting on the white evening-gown, having had her hair arranged by a hairdresser from Monte Carlo, she told herself she must behave as if she were grown up and not like a frightened school-girl.

Four times she had gone to the Salon to show her father and the Prince the clothes that *Madame* Yvette had brought with her and each time she had become more and more self-conscious.

It was undoubtedly because of the way in which the Prince looked at her and the things he said.

His words always seemed to have a double meaning and they often made her father laugh although she did not find them in the least funny.

"I must not make a fool of myself and shame Papa," Salena whispered as she looked in her mirror.

The maid who had helped her into her gown had been most complimentary.

"*M'mselle est ravissante!* like the lilies we grow for the market at Nice."

"The flower-market?" Salena asked. "I have heard of it and I would like to see it. The flowers must be beautiful."

"The carnations come from all along the coast to be sold there," the maid answered, "and lilies too—lilies for the Churches."

She smiled and made a gesture with her hand that was very French.

"Looking like that *M'mselle* should be in a shrine in one of our Churches not in the gaming-rooms in Monte Carlo."

"Are we going to Monte Carlo tonight?" Salena asked.

"*Mais oui, M'mselle*," the maid replied. "Every night, every afternoon, sometimes in the morning—everyone goes to the Casino. Me—I think it a waste of money."

"And so do I," Salena agreed.

At the same time, because she had heard so much about it she could not help thinking it would be rather exciting to see the Casino, even if she did not gamble.

There was a knock on the door and she knew it was her father who had promised he would take her downstairs with him.

Lord Cardenham was looking very rich and opulent with a pearl stud gleaming in the snowy expanse of his stiff shirt-front and a red carnation in his buttonhole.

He had always been a good-looking man and Salena thought it would be impossible for anyone to imagine that he was as penniless as he said he was.

"Ready, my dear?"

"Do I look all right, Papa?"

"I think the Prince has paid you enough compliments for it to be unnecessary for me to add to them," Lord Cardenham replied.

There was a note of satisfaction in his voice that Salena did not miss.

"How can we tell the Prince how grateful we are for his generosity?" Salena asked.

The maid had left the room and it was a question she had wanted to ask her father as soon as she had him alone.

"I am leaving that to you," he replied.

"To me, Papa? But I do not ... know what more ... to say."

"Then make yourself as pleasant as possible," Lord Cardenham advised. "Not many rich men would be so generous to someone they had never seen before and about whom they knew very little."

"I suspect, Papa ... that you have told him ... about me."

"I certainly described the circumstances in which you found yourself," her father agreed. "Russians are very sentimental, and as a child without a mother to advise her and a father with a hole in his pocket you are certainly pathetic, to say the least of it."

Salena gave a little sigh.

20

"The Prince has been very kind ... but I wish you had not had to ... ask him."

"He offered," Lord Cardenham said defensively.

Salena wanted to say that he had made it difficult for the Prince to do anything else, but she knew that any protestation she might make was just a waste of time.

Her father always had an eye to the main chance and it was difficult to blame him when they had invariably been on the point of bankruptcy.

"One thing is quite obvious," he went on, "and that is you pay with dressing, most especially when the gown is gilt-edged so to speak."

He put his arm round Salena, drew her to him and kissed her cheek.

"Now just express your gratitude to the Prince," he said, "and for God's sake, do not be tongue-tied. The trouble with Englishwomen is that they are never half as effusive as any other race."

"I will ... try to say the ... right thing," Salena murmured.

"That's a good girl," her father admonished. "Now let us go downstairs. I want to see *Madame* Versonne's face when she sees you. Be careful with that one—she is a regular tiger-cat."

"In what way?" Salena enquired. "I do not understand."

Lord Cardenham seemed about to explain, then he changed his mind.

"You will learn about these things soon enough," he said. "Just be yourself and keep your fingers crossed."

"For good luck, Papa?" Salena questioned.

"For good luck," Lord Cardenham repeated solemnly. "That is what I thought you had brought me when I saw you at the station, my poppet."

He took Salena down the broad stairs to the Salon.

As they entered it seemed to be filled with people.

21

There was the sound of laughter and the chatter of voices. Then Salena saw the Prince detach himself from a group to whom he was talking, among them *Madame* Versonne.

Salena had thought her beautiful when she saw her on the terrace but in evening-dress she was sensational!

Ostrich-feathers swirled round the hem of her gown and over her shoulders and made her appear as if she was rising from the waves of the sea.

Everything she wore was the colour of emeralds, complemented by an enormous necklace of the same precious stones.

Her dark hair was elaborately arranged on top of her head and in it she wore an osprey feather held by an enormous diamond and emerald brooch.

Salena was staring at her with so much admiration that she hardly realised the Prince was at her side, then hastily she curtseyed.

"You look just as I expected you to," he said.

"Thank you," she answered. "I do not know how to begin to tell you how grateful I am to Your Highness."

"Shall we keep what we have to say until later when we are alone?" the Prince asked.

"Yes ... of course," she answered, feeling that he did not wish the other people in the room to be aware of his generosity.

"Now I must introduce you to my friends."

He slipped his hand under Salena's elbow and moved her round the room.

There were so many new faces, so many almost unpronounceable names, so many titles, that at the end Salena knew no more about the guests than she had at the beginning.

The Prince turned away when someone else was announced and thankfully Salena moved to her father's side.

He was talking to *Madame* Versonne and she

thought as she joined them that the older woman's eyes hardened.

"Your daughter, My Lord," she said to Lord Cardenham, "should be attending a débutantes' Ball rather than making her début at the green baize tables."

"Salena will not be doing that," Lord Cardenham replied. "At the same time, I fear that débutantes are in somewhat short supply in Monte Carlo."

Madame Versonne laughed unpleasantly.

"They do not last long in any climate," she replied, "and inevitably they are more short-lived where there are Imperial eagles who peck at them."

There appeared to be a *double entendre* in what she said, which again Salena did not understand, but when *Madame* Versonne moved away from them in the direction of the Prince, Lord Cardenham said:

"I have warned you about that woman. You keep clear of her claws!"

"She does not seem to like me," Salena said. "I cannot think why, as she has never met me until now."

Lord Cardenham smiled.

"You do not have to search far for the reason."

"Tell me . . ." Salena began, but someone came up to speak to her father at that moment and he was unable to answer her.

She found herself at dinner seated between an elderly Russian who wanted only to talk of the different systems he had tried at the tables, and a Frenchman who paid her such elaborate and extravagant compliments that she found them almost ludicrous.

The food was delicious, the table laden not only with gold ornaments but also decorated with orchids.

Salena looked at it with awe.

She knew they were the most expensive flowers obtainable and it seemed incredible for them to be displayed in such profusion just on a dinner-table.

But then everything about the Prince seemed to

be ornate and overwhelmingly extravagant: the food, the wine, the jewels of the ladies, and the opulent splendour of the men.

It was a world in which Salena had imagined her father moving but which she had never seen before.

Even the cigars smoked by the gentlemen seemed longer and fatter than those she had noticed in the past.

She could not help feeling that it was incongruous for her and her father to be here when they themselves were so poor and had no idea where their next penny was coming from.

'I suppose it would be possible for Papa to work in order to earn money!' Salena thought to herself. 'But what could I do?'

She had often thought that she had no particular talent that was marketable.

She could draw and paint in an amateurish way, she could play the piano but she was certainly no virtuoso, and she was well aware that the only careers open to ladies were those of a Governess or a companion.

She gave a little sigh.

"I should hate to be either of those," she told herself, and wondered anxiously what the future held.

She could not help thinking that when they left the Villa they would have nowhere to go.

It would be less of a problem for her father.

There were always people who were prepared to invite him to stay with them, who would offer him what he would call "a bed to sleep on and a roof over his head," because he was so charming and such an asset to any party.

Salena remembered her mother saying once when her father had many invitations in which she was not included:

"You see, dearest, everyone wants an unattached man, especially one like your father; but a couple is much more trouble, particularly when they have nothing to offer in return."

"What could you offer in return?" Salena had asked.

"Hospitality," her mother replied. "If we had a house in the country or could give a Ball in London, or even large and amusing dinner-parties, it would be what your father calls a 'pay back.' But we can afford to do none of those things."

Salena had been very young at the time, but as she grew older she saw there were many occasions when even her mother and father's closest friends did not invite them to their parties.

Her mother took it as a matter of course, but it made her father swear and she knew he was frustrated at being left out.

'It is all a question of a "pay back"' Salena thought now. 'And how could I ever "pay back" for what anyone does for me?'

She looked down the long table to where the Prince was sitting at the far end with *Madame* Versonne on one side of him and another very attractive lady on the other.

They were making him laugh.

There was something in the attention they were giving him, the manner in which they bent towards him and in the expression in their eyes, which told Salena that this was the way they were showing their gratitude and perhaps their affection for him.

'That is what he ... expects,' she thought to herself.

The idea that he might expect it from her made her shiver.

Chapter Two

"No . . . Papa . . . I cannot do it . . . I cannot!"

Lord Cardenham walked to the window of Salena's bed-room and looked out at the sea.

He did not speak and after a moment Salena said nervously:

"I want to . . . please you, Papa, but I . . . hate the Prince. I cannot explain . . . but he makes me feel . . . frightened . . . there is something in the way he . . . looks at me."

It was not only the way he looked at her. It was when he touched her that she felt a revulsion run through her, as if there was a snake moving over her skin.

He seemed always to be near her, so that his hand touched hers or their shoulders brushed against each other's.

She had had the feeling for the last week that he was encroaching nearer and nearer and at night she fell asleep to wake with a start because he haunted her dreams.

She was well aware that *Madame* Versonne looked at her with hatred and she addressed her in a more and more aggressive manner, which made Salena shrink within herself and try to be as inconspicuous as possible.

But now, incredibly, unbelievably, her father had said that the Prince wished to marry her.

"He is ... old, Papa," she protested piteously as still her father did not answer her. "Of course I would like to be married ... someday ... but I want to fall in ... love and with a ... young man."

"Young men have no money!"

The words came harshly to Lord Cardenham's lips, then he turned round and there was an expression in his eyes that Salena had never seen before.

"Do not imagine I have not thought about this," he said. "I have lain awake at night trying to find another way out, but quite frankly, my dear, there is nothing else we can do."

Salena looked at him, her eyes dark and frightened in her pale face.

"You mean, Papa, that I must ... marry the Prince because he is ... rich?"

"He has today settled two thousand pounds a year on you," Lord Cardenham answered, "and you are intelligent enough to realise what that means to both of us."

Salena made a little sound but did not say anything, and her father went on:

"Two thousand pounds a year is a considerable amount of money, besides which ..."

He paused, looking embarrassed, and Salena said softly:

"He is giving you ... something ... too, Papa."

"He is giving me enough to pay my debts and prevent me from feeling as desperate as I have for a long time about the future."

There was silence for a moment. Then he went on:

"It is a question really of asking you to do this, Salena, or I might as well shoot myself and get it over."

"What do you ... mean, Papa?"

"I mean that if I cannot pay up what I owe, it will result in my being sued, and the inevitable publicity would, in one particular instance, compel me to resign from my Clubs."

Barbara Cartland

Salena was well aware what this penalty would mean.

Her father's life, when he was not staying with his friends, centred round the two exclusive and smart London Clubs to which he belonged.

"Have you ... done something ... wrong, Papa?"

"You, and doubtless your mother, would have considered it wrong," her father replied harshly. "Shall I say I took a gamble which sailed pretty near the wind and I lost!"

"You really ... mean that if I do not ... marry the Prince you would be in ... serious trouble?"

"Very serious!" Lord Cardenham said gravely.

Salena gave a deep sigh which seemed to come from the very depths of her heart.

She might have guessed, she thought, when her father first told her that the Prince wished to marry her that there would be no escape.

Because the idea horrified her and made her feel that she could not contemplate what lay ahead, she rose to run to her father like a small frightened child.

He put his arms round her and held her close against him. Then he said in a voice that seemed to be strangled in his throat:

"I am a rotten father to you, my poppet, but at least you will be safe, whatever happens in the future."

Salena's impulse was to reply that nothing worse or more terrifying could happen to her than having to be the Prince's wife.

But she knew that her father was suffering and because she loved him she managed to say with a courage she was far from feeling:

"I will try ... Papa, to behave as you would ... wish me to."

Her father put his hand under her chin and turned her face up to his.

He looked down at her for a long moment, then said almost as if he was speaking to himself:

28

"If only there had been more time—if only we could have waited! There might have been someone else."

Salena said nothing because she did not think an answer was expected of her, but she could not help recalling how many men had paid her compliments since she had come to Monte Carlo.

Every night when they went to the Casino and she had kept close to her father's side while they watched the gambling, there had always been men he knew who came up to him quite obviously with the desire to be introduced to her.

Although this had made her feel shy and she had not always known how to reply, what they said did not make her shrink away in disgust and revulsion, as did the flowery sentences which fell from the Prince's lips.

One reason why Salena enjoyed going to the Casino was that as soon as they arrived, the Prince would be hurried away to the Baccarat-tables by *Madame* Versonne.

She would sit beside him and play with his money, and the Prince would concentrate, like the other immensely rich men at the table, at trying to beat the bank.

Her father had explained to Salena who many of the other players were. When she asked innocently why such wealthy men should have nothing better to do than want to win more money, he answered:

"There is very little sense in gambling, but it gives those who are satiated with luxury a thrill which is irresistible."

Salena knew that he himself was longing to play but could not afford it.

Instead he would stake a few francs on the roulette-table or occasionally try his luck at trente-et-quarante.

It made her feel so anxious and so frightened in case he should lose that it was almost an agony to watch the turn of the card or the fall of the little white ball in the roulette-wheel.

Then inevitably would come the moment when the Prince would join them, his eyes on her face, his hand reaching out to touch her.

She would long to run away and hide, only to remember almost despairingly that he had paid for the gown she was wearing and therefore must express her gratitude by being polite to him.

Because everyone staying at the Villa was a foreigner, Salena would long for an English face and to talk to someone of the same nationality as herself.

One evening a man who was obviously English nodded to her father as he passed through the rooms.

He was tall, broad-shouldered, and fair-skinned, although his hair was a dark brown.

He was as smartly dressed as every other man in the Casino, yet he gave the impression of wearing his clothes casually, as if they were a part of him.

"Good-evening, Cardenham," the Englishman said.

"I hope it will be," her father joked. "But it is too soon yet to tell."

The Englishman knew he spoke of his gambling and laughed.

"Who was that?" Salena enquired.

She watched the tall man with the broad shoulders as he moved through the throng of glittering women and men who seemed somehow stuffed into their evening-clothes.

"That is the Duke of Templecombe," her father replied.

"It was his yacht we saw when I arrived," Salena said, a little lilt in her voice.

"Yes—the *Aphrodite*," her father answered. "I would like to look it over if I had the chance. I hear it is the most up-to-date vessel of its kind in the whole of Europe."

"I would like to see it too," Salena said.

But although she looked for the Duke, hoping her father would get into conversation with him, he was not at the Casino the next night or the night after.

"There is something I have to tell you..." her father was saying.

She knew by the stiffness of the way he was holding himself, or perhaps it was the tone of his voice, that he was embarrassed.

"What is it, Papa?"

"The Prince wishes you to marry him at once!"

"At once? Oh no, Papa! That is ... impossible!"

"He insists," Lord Cardenham said, "and frankly, Salena, I need the money he has promised me."

"How is it ... possible? How can we be married so ... quickly?"

She asked the question pathetically and added:

"What will ... *Madame* Versonne ... say?"

It had been very obvious, even to someone who was as inexperienced as Salena, that *Madame* Versonne looked on the Prince as her special property.

She moved everywhere beside him, while her proprietary manner and the way she constituted herself as the hostess in the Villa had made Salena feel, despite the way the Prince looked at her, that it was *Madame* Versonne whom he intended to marry.

She had heard no-one discuss such an idea, but many of the guests spoke to one another in Russian, which she did not understand. Anyway, it had never crossed her mind that the Prince was an eligible bachelor.

For the moment she felt stunned by the suggestion that she should marry him, and it was even more incredible that this marriage should take place at once.

"But ... how ... how is it ... possible?" she asked again.

"The Prince has thought of everything," Lord Cardenham replied, "and he is at this moment informing those who are staying in the house that his personal servant has a virulent form of scarlet fever."

He paused before he continued:

"His Highness is therefore arranging for everyone to move to the Hôtel de Paris. He had taken over two floors, and I am to play host until you are married and have left on your honeymoon."

"B-but ... Papa ..." Salena began to expostulate. Then she realised that there was nothing she could say, and her voice died away.

"The Prince is pretending that as he has been in close contact with his servant, he must be isolated for several weeks."

Lord Cardenham went on:

"The Villa is supposed to be fumigated and in a few days the party will return but by that time you will both have left."

He walked again to the window as he added:

"God knows how I am to break the news that he has left to *Madame* Versonne. She will be furious! At the same time, the Prince will undoubtedly placate her extremely generously."

"But ... what am I ... going to do? And where will the ... P-Prince be taking me?" Salena asked.

"You will be married secretly here this evening in the Villa, so that no-one will be aware of it," Lord Cardenham said. "You must understand, Salena, that the Prince is supposed to ask permission of the Tsar but he says it would take too long for him to journey to Russia and back again."

"S-surely it would be ... better for him to do that?" Salena asked quickly.

"It would not be better for me!" Lord Cardenham retorted.

"No ... no, of course not, Papa. I had forgotten about that," Salena said hastily.

"You do understand the need for secrecy?" her father asked. "Besides, it would be extremely uncomfortable for you to face *Madame* Versonne and all the comments his other friends will make."

"Yes ... of course ... I have no wish to ... listen to them."

She told herself that she was in fact frightened of *Madame* Versonne, and everything that was sensitive in her shrank from seeing the anger and envy in the other women's eyes.

All those in the house-party were, she thought, the sort of ladies with whom her mother would have put on a cold air and been very quiet and frigid in their company.

Her mother had never criticised her father's friends, but sometimes when they had come to the house Salena had known that there was an atmosphere of hostility that was unmistakable.

It was then that her mother became stiff and quiet, very unlike her smiling, fascinating self.

All the women here seemed to Salena, when she compared them with her mother, somehow vulgar, or perhaps the right word was "fast."

"Men may like her," she had heard her mother say once of some lady of whom she disapproved, "because she is fast in her ways, but as far as I am concerned, I hope I never see her again!"

Salena was well aware that her mother would have said that of everyone with whom she had been acquainted since arriving at Monte Carlo, and most especially of *Madame* Versonne.

At the same time, she tried not to criticise because she knew it would only upset her father, and they had nowhere else to go.

But now she thought that perhaps for the rest of her life she would be forced to associate with such women and how unpleasant it would be.

It was not that they were all so vitriolic and disdainful as *Madame* Versonne.

It was, she sensed, their insincerity and the manner in which they gushed over the Prince and every other man, including her father.

It was as if they were acting a part, but underneath all the pretence Salena somehow fancied they were just grasping and grabbing at everything they could get and had no real affection for anyone.

"No, Papa," she said aloud, "I would hate ... for anyone here in the Villa to know about my ... wedding."

Then she added:

"Must it ... really be so soon as ... tonight?"

"What is the point of waiting?" her father asked. "The Prince has arranged everything so that there will be no time for people to question his arrangements."

"But you will ... stay with me, Papa?"

I am afraid that is impossible," her father replied. "The Prince is alleging that everyone who has not come in contact with the afflicted servant is safe so long as they leave at once."

"B-but ... Papa ... I c-cannot be left ... alone!"

"I will stay with you for as long as I can," her father replied. "We shall obviously travel in several carriages, and I will be the last to leave."

"Surely ... everyone will ... expect me to be with ... you?"

"The Prince has thought of that too," Lord Cardenham replied. "You have been asked by some school-friends to stay at another Villa and that I thought it would be nice for you to be with young people."

Salena thought that this was what she really would like—to be with her friends rather than left alone with the repulsive elderly man who was to be her husband.

"I am sorry, my dear," her father was saying, "sorry this has been such a shock. But believe me, if the Prince had not offered for you, I have not the slightest idea what I should have done to save us both from sleeping in the gutter!"

Lord Cardenham looked towards the wardrobe. It was open and he could see the dozens of gowns

34

that *Madame* Yvette had supplied for Salena hanging inside.

New ones arrived day after day, and with them came boxes filled with lace-trimmed nightgowns and petticoats and silk stockings, and slippers dyed to match the gowns and wraps edged with fur.

At first Salena had tried to protest that it was too much, that she did not need so many things.

But her father had been quite cross with her and so she tried to accept gracefully what she was given and express in stumbling words her gratitude.

As if her father knew what she was thinking, he put his hand now into his pocket and drew out a jewel-box.

"His Highness asked me to give you this," he said. "He thought it would please you and mitigate the shock of everything happening so quickly."

He held out the small leather case to Salena and it was with an effort that she forced herself to take it.

She guessed what it contained, and thought it was a chain binding her to a man she hated.

Slowly, with fingers that trembled, she opened the box. Inside was a huge ruby ring surrounded by diamonds.

It had an antique setting, and her father explained:

"It belongs, I think, to the Prince's family collection, and I can tell you one thing, Salena—he will load you with jewels because he is completely and absolutely infatuated with you."

Salena did not answer. She was looking at the ruby, thinking that it seemed to glow with an evil fire and she hated it.

"In fact, the Prince said to me," Lord Cardenham continued, "that he had never in his life been so captivated or enraptured by any woman."

As if he was speaking to himself he added:

"I think he would have paid any price for you."

Salena looked at him and said quietly:

"He is ... buying me, Papa, and it makes me feel ..., ashamed that he has paid so much ... already."

"There is no reason for you to feel ashamed," her father replied angrily. "You are beautiful, Salena —beautiful, young, and untouched. Any man would be proud to own you."

He looked at her and sighed.

"If only we had more time!"

Salena put the ruby ring down on the dressing-table and closed the box.

"When am I to be ... ready?" she asked.

"Because the Prince is anxious to be quite certain that everyone has left the Villa, you will ... not be married until after dinner. It will take time for the ladies to pack, and of course he has other arrangements to make."

"What are ... they?" Salena asked nervously.

"I think he intends to take you away tomorrow in his yacht," Lord Cardenham replied. "I suggested you might like to see the Greek Islands. They are very beautiful at this time of the year."

Salena's eyes lit up for a moment. She had always longed to see the Greek Islands. Then she remembered who would be with her and her vision of them suddenly seemed to be covered in darkness.

"The Prince will explain everything to you himself," Lord Cardenham said, "but I think you would be wise to stay here in your bed-room until dinner-time. Everyone is bound to have gone by then."

"Do not ... go until you ... have to, Papa. Please!" Salena begged.

"No, of course not," he answered, "but I would like a drink, and I suggest that we sit on the balcony of the next room. I know it is unoccupied."

He opened the door to look outside in an almost conspiratorial manner, than beckoned to Salena to follow him.

They went into the next room, which looked over the garden towards the sea.

It was rather larger than the one occupied by Salena, and outside the window was a large balcony with the awnings down to keep the room cool.

Lord Cardenham rang the bell and when a servant appeared he ordered champagne. Then he walked out onto the balcony and Salena followed him.

"A drink will do you good," he said. "I know this has been a shock, and there is nothing like champagne to make one feel that things are not as bad as they appear."

Salena did not answer.

She was fighting an impulse to plead once more with her father, to beg him to save her, to let her run away alone so that she could hide.

But she knew she could not ruin him through sheer selfishness.

Her mother had said to her so often:

"Men are like children, Salena, and we have to look after them, even though they think they are looking after us."

"Do you really look after Papa?" Salena had asked curiously.

"In a thousand different ways of which he has no idea," her mother replied. "In fact, darling, I do not mind telling you he would get into a lot of trouble if I was not there."

That, Salena thought, was exactly what had happened. Her mother was dead and her father on his own had not been able to look after himself.

'I have to save him,' she thought, 'however hard it may be. I must save him for Mama's sake.'

Because she knew perceptively that he was feeling uncomfortable and perhaps miserable, she put out her hand and slipped it into his.

"I am sure it will be ... all right, Papa," she said as if she was consoling him.

"I am praying that it will be all right for you," Lord Cardenham answered. "Remember, dearest, that you will have money of your own and jewels.

That is what every woman wants, what every woman should have."

"Where will I . . . live?" Salena asked.

She had a sudden fear that the Prince might take her away to Russia and she would not see her father again.

"I do not know what the Prince's plans are," Lord Cardenham replied, "but I imagine that when your honeymoon is over you will go to Paris. He has a magnificent house there, but I am quite sure he will be only too glad to take you anywhere."

"I want to be near . . . you."

"I expect that can be arranged," her father replied. "I have always got on well with Serge—in fact, he counts me as one of his closest friends."

"Then will you ask him, Papa, if you can join us as soon as possible?

"I shall have to be tactful about it," Lord Cardenham replied. "I have a feeling that the Prince will want to have you to himself."

Salena shuddered, but aloud she said:

"How long do . . . honeymoons usually . . . last, Papa?"

"It depends," Lord Cardenham answered evasively.

She had the feeling it would depend on whether she amused the Prince or not. If he found her boring, he would want to return to the chattering, laughing people who entertained him.

"Perhaps it will be only a week or so before I see you again, Papa," she said.

"I hope so," her father replied, "but naturally you will not be able to come here."

Salena thought that that was because *Madame* Versonne would still be the Prince's guest.

It seemed strange that she should want to stay on if he was married, but she thought it best not to ask too many questions and she was well aware that her father was embarrassed by them.

"We have had so ... little time together, Papa," she said. "I had hoped that I could live with you and look ... after you as Mama used to do."

"That is what I wanted too," her father replied, "and if I had not been a damned fool it might have been possible for a little while. But being without money is hell! It is no use pretending, Salena, that one can manage without it, because one cannot!"

"No, Papa."

"And that is why the Prince has solved our immediate problems, and we have to settle the future in a different way from what I anticipated."

"What did you anticipate, Papa?"

"There is no point in talking about it now," her father said quickly. "You will be secure, Salena, and, as I have said, that is the only thing that matters."

She could not help feeling that she would be very insecure with the Prince, whatever her position financially. Yet she knew it was no use saying such things.

It had all been arranged and because she loved her father there was nothing she could do but acquiesce and try not to feel almost sick with fear, knowing that in a few hours' time she would be married to the Prince.

Then, she supposed, he would touch her and kiss her!

She looked out at the blue of the Mediterranean and wished she could swim away towards the misty horizon.

It was as if all her ideals and all the fantasies she had had about love and marriage were disappearing to where the sea joined the sky.

She had dreamt that one day she might meet a man who would be as good-looking as her father had been when he was young, and he would fall in love with her and she with him.

It would all be very wonderful and she would live happily ever afterwards like the end of the fairy-stories.

Barbara Cartland

But instead . . .

She felt a pain inside her breast which had been there ever since her father had told her she was to be married to the Prince, stabbing her with a physical agony that seemed to intensify with every moment that passed.

The champagne arrived and her father made her drink a little of it, but instead of sweeping away her fears it seemed to multiply them.

Everywhere she looked she seemed to see the Prince's eyes with an expression in them which was terrifying.

Finally she went back to her bed-room and looked again at the ruby ring he had given her and she thought it too held the same expression.

Her father was almost casual in his leave-taking, and she knew it was because he was afraid she would make a scene and also because he too was upset at saying good-bye.

"Take care of yourself, my poppet," he said almost cheerfully. "Remember, it is uncomfortable and degrading living without money, and pretty gowns and glittering jewels make up for a great many other things."

She knew he was referring to her feelings for the Prince.

When he had left her bed-room, shutting the door behind him, she had to bite her lips not to cry out after him.

It took an iron control to prevent herself from pulling open the door and telling him that after all it was impossible; that she would do anything, go anywhere he liked, but she could not, *would* not, marry the Prince.

Instead she ran to her bed and flung herself face downwards on it.

With a superhuman effort she refrained from crying, even though the tears pricked her eyes. Then she lay listening for the sound of the last carriage, carrying her father away from the Villa.

She had a feeling that he would be telling himself all the way to Monte Carlo that nothing mattered except that she had two thousand pounds a year for the rest of her life.

How could it matter so much when the Prince was so wealthy and she would be his wife?

It was understandable, she supposed, that her father was safe-guarding her against the day when the Prince became bored with her and might then not be so generous.

It was difficult not to hope and even pray that the day in question would come quickly.

"Perhaps after all he will not want me, and decide he would rather marry someone like *Madame* Versonne," Salena said aloud.

Then she knew she was only daydreaming, telling herself stories as she had done ever since as a child she had imagined she was taking part in strange and exciting adventures.

Always the Good Fairy, the White Knight, or Prince Charming rescued her at the last moment from the gnomes, the dragon, or the wicked giant.

But this time there would be no rescue and the Prince was certainly not the man she had seen in her dreams.

A maid came to inform her that dinner was at eight o'clock and to prepare Salena's bath.

While it was being got ready a gown-box arrived from *Madame* Yvette; it contained, as Salena might have expected, a wedding-gown.

It was even more beautiful than all the beautiful gowns *Madame* had made for her, but she felt as if it were a shroud.

The box also contained a lace veil and a wreath of artificial orange blossoms.

Salena remembered that in her dream-stories she had always worn a wreath of real flowers.

'But then my marriage was one of love,' she thought. 'This is wrong and false!'

As false as the orange-blossom buds, which

looked somehow coarse and garish when compared to the flowers outside in the garden.

However, she did not speak but let the maid dress her almost as if she were a doll, without any feelings.

"Am I to wear the veil now?" Salena asked, and she thought her voice sounded strange even to herself.

"I think His Highness expects it, *M'mselle*," the maid replied.

She was excited at the idea of dressing a bride and chattered away, although it seemed to Salena that her voice came from a far distance.

"Earlier this year, before I came to work for His Highness," she was saying, "my sister was married. It was not a grand ceremony, but such a happy one! Everyone in the neighbourhood came to the Church, and because we could not afford to entertain so many they all contributed a little towards the wedding-feast. We laughed, we sang, we danced. It was the happiest day I have ever known."

"And this is my unhappiest," Salena wanted to say.

Instead, she watched her reflection in the mirror as the maid arranged the veil over her fair hair and fixed it in place with the wreath of orange blossoms.

"*M'mselle est très belle!*" she exclaimed in almost awe-struck tones.

Salena rose to her feet.

"It must be nearly nine o'clock. I will go downstairs now."

She would have left the room but the maid cried:

"One moment, *M'mselle!* You have forgotten your engagement-ring! His Highness will be disappointed if you do not wear it for dinner."

"Y-yes ... of course ..." Salena said dully.

She let the maid slip the ring on the third finger of her left hand.

Against the whiteness of her gown she thought it

looked like a drop of blood. Hastily she walked downstairs.

The Prince was waiting for her in the Salon and she realised as she entered that the whole room had been filled with white flowers.

He was in evening-dress and two huge diamond studs glittered on his shirt-front.

For a moment when she entered he stood looking at her. Then as her eyes fell before his he walked forward to take her hand.

"This is the moment I have been looking forward to," he said.

He kissed the back of her hand, then turned it over, and she felt his lips on her palm.

There was something hard and greedy about them, something which made her want to snatch her hand away from him.

'I must behave properly. I must behave as Papa would wish,' Salena told herself.

The Prince must have known she was afraid, for she was trembling, but, taking her hand in his, he drew her from the Salon into the small room next door.

They were not dining, Salena realised, in the large Dining-Room which they had used ever since she had come to the Villa, but in a small room.

It had sometimes been used at breakfastime, but now it had been converted into a veritable bower of white flowers.

There were white orchids on the table and the fragrance of lilies was almost overpowering.

"Our first meal alone together," the Prince said as they sat down. "I cannot tell you, my adorable little Salena, how boring I have found the people who have kept us apart."

If he had been bored he certainly had not shown it, she thought, remembering the loud laughter that had seemed to surround him on every occasion this past week.

"I asked your father to arrange that our mar-

43

riage should be kept a close secret," the Prince went on, "because I thought we would have no desire to listen to the gushing congratulations of others but would much rather be alone."

He paused to add impressively:

"I cannot begin to tell how much I have wanted to talk to you."

"What ... about?" Salena questioned, feeling she was expected to answer him.

"There could be only one subject," the Prince replied with a smile, "and that, of course, is love!"

The way he said the word made Salena hastily take a little sip of the champagne that stood beside her, as if she felt it would fortify her.

He was speaking in English, and, as the servants were French, she hoped they did not understand. But there could be no misunderstanding the passionate note in the Prince's voice or the expression in his eyes.

"I fell in love with you as soon as I saw you," he answered, "and I told myself you would be mine."

His eyes were on her face as he went on:

"You are so young, so innocent, and so very desirable, but I swore that no-one and nothing should stand between us—and let me tell you, Salena, I always get what I want."

Now there was a fire in his eyes and his voice deepened until it seemed to Salena to be almost like the snarl of an animal.

"I have never ... known anyone ... Russian before," she said quickly. "I hope you will tell me about ... Russia and your ... home there."

"Russia is far away," the Prince answered, "and we are close to each other. That is more important at the moment."

"But naturally I am ... interested in your ... country and ... of course your ... people."

Salena hesitated a moment before she went on:

"I have heard there is much ... suffering in Russia and ... poverty."

"That is the sort of ridiculous story spread about

by people who do not know our great land," the Prince replied. "Perhaps one day you will see it for yourself. In the meantime, we have other things to talk about."

Salena was relieved when he said "perhaps." That meant that he did not intend to take her to Russia—not, at any rate, for the moment.

It meant that she would not lose contact with her father, and it was a consolation in itself to know he was only a few miles away.

She had seen the Hôtel de Paris when she visited the Casino, and she knew he would enjoy the opportunity of playing host when he did not have to foot the bill.

"What are you thinking about?" the Prince asked.

"I was thinking of Papa."

"You need not worry about your father. As I expect he told you, I have looked after him."

"You have been . . . very kind."

"Do you really think so? And do you think also that I have been kind to you?"

"Very kind . . . and I am very . . . grateful," Salena said. "I have not . . . thanked you yet for . . . the ring."

She put out her hand as she spoke and the ruby glinted at her.

In the candlelight it seemed, as she thought absurdly, to be like the "evil eye" that she had read of in books written about the East.

"I have other jewels to give you," the Prince said. "Necklaces which I will clasp round your throat and brooches I will pin between your soft breasts."

A little shiver of horror seemed to run down Salena's spine.

"Y-you are . . . very . . . kind," she murmured again.

"It is difficult for me to be anything else to you," he said, "but you must also be kind to me."

"Yes . . . of course . . ."

"It will be very exciting to teach you about love,"

45

the Prince said, "in fact it will be the most exciting
thing I have done for a long time."

It seemed to Salena as if the meal were in-
terminable, but at last it was over. Then the Prince
sharply asked a question of one of the servants.

"He is waiting, Your Highness," was the reply.

The Prince turned to Salena and offered her his
arm.

She put her hand on it, feeling as if he were
taking her to the guillotine.

It flashed through her mind that it was exactly
how the aristocrats who had met their deaths in the
Place de la Révolution had felt when there had been
no way of escape.

If they had to die, they did so proudly.

Salena put up her chin, and now the Prince was
taking her through the hall and along a passage
which she knew led to his private apartments.

Unlike his guests, the Prince slept on the same
floor as the Salon, and Salena knew from something
her father had said that his rooms opened onto the
terrace.

The passage ended with a door, which was
opened for them by a servant, and then the Prince
led her through yet another door.

Salena found that she was in a room which had
been arranged as a Chapel.

There were the seven silver sanctuary lamps
which she knew were a part of the Russian Orthodox
faith, and standing in front of an altar was a Priest
who had a long beard and wore a huge crucifix on his
black robe.

The Chapel was lit only by candles. The air was
thick with incense and there was a profusion of
white flowers.

There were two white satin cushions on the floor
and Salena and the Prince knelt on them.

The Priest began what sounded like a long
prayer, but, as he spoke in Russian, Salena had no

idea what he said. When he finished, the Prince took her hand in his and drew off the ruby ring to replace it with a gold band.

Then the Priest put his hand over theirs and blessed them, and the Prince rose to his feet.

"Now we are married, Salena," he said, and drew her with what seemed impatience from the Chapel.

Outside in the corridor, he opened another door and now Salena found herself in a large, beautiful Sitting-Room.

"You are my wife," the Prince said, "and at last I can tell you of my love and we shall not be interrupted."

"Can I . . . first look at your room?" Salena asked. "I have never . . . been here . . . before."

As if the Prince knew she was evading him, there was a smile on his lips as he said:

"Let me show you your bed-room. At the moment that room is more important to us than any other."

Because there was nothing she could say, Salena followed him through another door and found herself in a large room with long French windows opening onto the terrace.

Below in the garden she could see the fountain glowing iridescent through lights skilfully concealed amongst the flowers.

The stars were shining brightly in the dark sky, but it was difficult to look at anything but the large bed, which seemed, to Salena's imagination, almost to fill the room.

There were silk curtains draping the bed, and the sheets were drawn back, and she dared not think to herself what was implied.

"Why do we wait?" she heard the Prince ask. "I will ring for your maid. Then when you are in bed I will come back and we can be alone."

He rang the bell as he spoke and, as if she had been waiting for the summons, the maid who had looked after Salena since she had first come to the Villa appeared.

The Prince kissed Salena's hand and said:

"Do not keep me waiting long, my beautiful one."

He walked back into the Sitting-Room, the diamond studs in his shirt glittering as he went.

"His Highness is an impatient bridegroom," the maid said with relish, savouring the drama of the moment.

She took off Salena's wreath and veil and undid her wedding-gown at the back.

Feeling as if she were in a dream, Salena hardly noticed what was happening until she was wearing a nightgown so elaborate that it might have been a ball-dress.

Of the finest handkerchief lawn, it was inset with real Valenciennes lace, and the same lace, only deeper, bordered the hem and the sleeves.

"Let me brush Your Highness's hair," the maid suggested.

Salena turned towards the dressing-table as if she could no longer think but must do what was expected of her automatically.

Then as she sat down she saw there was a letter propped against her hair-brushes, and realised from the handwriting that it was from her father.

She tore it open. Her father had written:

My Dearest,
     This is just a line to tell you how much I love you and how much I want your happiness. Send me a note when you can to tell me you forgive me, and that you still care for your very affectionate and penitent father.

                              Cardenham

Salena felt a surge of warmth rise within her as she read the note through twice.

She felt she understood what her father was trying to say and how it really worried him that in
order to save them both she must do what she hated
doing.

She rose from the dressing-table.

"Wait one moment," she said to her maid. "I will
just write to my father, and perhaps if it is not too
late someone could take it to him in Monte Carlo?"

"Yes, of course, Your Highness," the maid replied.
"It will be quite easy for one of the grooms to carry it."

Standing in the corner of the room was a *Secrétaire.* It was an attractive piece of inlaid furniture,
but it was closed.

Salena tried to open it.

"It is locked," she said to the maid, "and I want
some writing-paper."

"I expect the key is in a drawer, Your Highness,"
the maid replied. "If not, I'll go and ask the House-
keeper."

"Let me look first," Salena said.

She opened one of the small drawers and discovered the key in a corner of it.

Pulling out the two struts of wood which sup-
ported the flap, Salena unlocked the desk and found,
as she had expected, that inside there was a blotter,
writing-paper, and envelopes.

She put the blotter down on the flap and as she
did so she saw there were two framed photographs
pushed against the ink-pot.

She picked one up to look at it.

It was a picture of an attractive woman in an
evening-gown, wearing the most magnificent jewels.

Salena wondered vaguely who she was, then saw
an inscription on the photograph in French:

To Serge—from his loving wife, Olga

Salena stared at it in astonishment.

No-one had ever told her, she thought, that the

Prince was a widower. It seemed strange that her father had never mentioned it.

There was another photograph, and without really thinking she picked it up.

It was the same woman, but this time there were four children forming a group with her, the eldest looking about sixteen.

The writing was in the same hand.

*To Darling Serge—from Olga and his loving
family—Christmas, 1902*

For what seemed a long time Salena stared at the picture.

Then slowly, as if she were groping her way through a fog, the explanation of what she held in her hand came to her like a far-away voice.

The secrecy over the wedding—her father's insistence that she would be safe whatever happened in the future—the way she had been kept from speaking to anyone who might have revealed the truth . . .

Vaguely at the back of her mind she remembered hearing that the Russian aristocrats who came to Monte Carlo left their wives at home so that they could enjoy themselves *en garçon*.

Now she recalled, again as if it came from a long way away, that in the Russian solemnisation of marriage the bride and bridegroom had crowns held over their heads.

This had not happened at their ceremony and she suspected that the Priest had not been a real one, or else the service he had performed over them had not been one of marriage.

She could not move—she just sat staring at the photograph of the four children and the woman with the attractive face.

Behind her, the maid said in a frightened tone:

"What is the matter, Your Highness? Has something upset you?"

"I am . . . all right," Salena said after a moment. "Leave me."

"But, Your Highness, your hair . . . !"

"Please leave me!"

"I will be waiting for a summons, Your Highness."

Salena did not answer. She heard the maid close the door, then she rose to stand still looking at the photograph she held in her hand.

It might have been a long time, or it might have been a few seconds—she had no idea—before the door opened and the Prince came into the room.

He had changed from his evening-clothes and was wearing a thin, Oriental-looking cotton robe which was fashionable in the South of France when it was hot.

Because he wore nothing round his neck he looked different, and at the same time older.

His elegance had gone. He was just a heavy, middle-aged man. Only his eyes remained unchanged, and the passion flared into them as he saw Salena's body thinly veiled by her diaphanous nightgown.

"You are ready for me, my beautiful bride?"

"Yes, I am . . . ready for you," Salena answered. "Will you please . . . explain this?"

She held out the photograph as she spoke and saw him start. Then a frown replaced the look of excitement on his face.

"Where did you get that?" he asked. "Who gave it to you?"

"No-one gave it to me," Salena answered. "I found it in the *Secrétaire*."

"The fools! The imbeciles!" the Prince cried angrily.

He snatched the photograph out of her hand and threw it with a crash into the corner of the room.

"That does not concern us!"

"It concerns me," Salena replied. "I am not . . . married to you. You know I am . . . not."

"What does that matter?" the Prince asked. "I love you and I will teach you to love me."

"Do you really think I would let you . . . touch me now that I know you were only . . . pretending to make me your . . . wife?"

"I have told you that is of no consequence," the Prince answered. "I will look after you—you will have all the money you want—more jewels than you can . . ."

"No!" Salena interrupted. "You have a wife. You have children. It is wicked and wrong to say such things to . . . me when you . . . belong to them."

"I belong to you and you belong to me," the Prince said.

He came towards her and Salena screamed.

"You are not to . . . touch me! I am . . . leaving now! I am going to . . . find Papa."

"Do you think your father wants you?" the Prince asked. "He is very satisfied with what I have paid him for you, and you will soon be satisfied too, my pretty little dove."

"No . . . no!" Salena screamed.

She would have run from the room but the Prince caught her in his arms and pulled her against him.

She fought him frantically—fought with her hands, her arms, and her feet.

She was small and delicate, and yet it was impossible for him to hold her still when she struggled against him so ferociously.

She hurt him and wincing he loosened his arms.

"I see you must be treated like a Russian peasant," he said. "Then you shall learn who is the master."

He turned as he spoke and went back into the Sitting-Room.

For a moment Salena was so breathless, and had

been so intent on fighting desperately to be free of him, that she could not realise he had left her.

She stared incredulously across the room, but as she turned towards the door which led to the passage, he returned.

There was a cruel smile on his lips and an expression on his face that seemed to her so menacing and so terrifying that for the moment it was impossible for her to move.

Then she saw that he held in his hand a long, thin riding-whip.

She stared at it in silence as he came towards her, and only as he put out his arm did she scream and try to move.

But she was too late!

He flung her forward onto the bed, and the next moment she felt the whip strike her across the shoulders.

She screamed and when he had only struck her three times she managed to struggle to her feet and evade him.

He caught at the back of her nightgown and it tore in his hands as she ran across the room, trying to reach the door into the Sitting-Room.

She stumbled and only saved herself from falling by holding on to the *Secrétaire*. She clutched at it and felt something hard beneath the fingers of her right hand.

She felt it could be a weapon of some sort with which she could strike at her pursuer.

But before she could realise what it was, the Prince picked her up from behind, carried her back to the bed, and threw her face-downwards on it.

Her nose was buried in the sheets, and as she gasped for breath the whip came down on her back.

Now as she screamed the Prince used the whip relentlessly, each blow biting into her bare flesh like a tongue of fire searing its way into her consciousness.

Everything seemed to go hazy, and although

someone was screaming, she did not even know it was herself.

Then as her voice died into silence, the Prince, breathing heavily yet making a grunt of satisfaction, turned her over.

She was helpless in his hands, lying almost unconscious on the bed, her eyes closed.

She was holding in her right hand, hidden in the folds of her nightgown, the paper-knife she had inadvertently picked up from the *Secrétaire*. In her agony she had gripped it tightly, and when the Prince turned her over it pointed upwards.

He did not see it.

With a sound of triumph he flung himself on top of her, and the stiletto-like point pierced him in the stomach.

He gave a cry that was hoarse and broken as he rolled off her, clutching at the knife.

"You have—killed me! I am—dead! Fetch the Doctor! Save me—God, save me!"

Salena sat up and saw the Prince lying half-naked beside her, his fingers round the jewelled handle of the paper-knife, blood pouring from the wound which it had inflicted onto the white cover of the bed.

"You have killed me! You have—killed me!" he said accusingly in French. "Help! Help!"

The last sound seemed lost in the thickness of his throat, and to Salena's frightened eyes he was dying.

Slowly, almost as if she could not realise that she was free to do so, she moved from the bed onto the floor.

"I—am—dying!" the Prince gasped, and then his eyes closed.

His fingers were stained with blood and there was a crimson pool beside him.

With a sound of sheer terror Salena ran through the open window onto the terrace.

She saw the fountain glittering beneath her, and

hardly aware of what she was doing she sped towards the steps that led down into the garden.

Her bare feet made hardly a sound on the white marble. Then she was on the green lawn, passing the fountain and running through the trees until she reached the end of the promontory.

Just for a moment she hesitated, looking down at the waves swirling below her against the grey rocks.

She threw herself forward, and felt the shock of the cold water in her eyes.

Then she started to swim frantically, wildly, out to sea. . . .

Chapter Three

The Duke of Templecombe was winning, and the pile of gold louis in front of him multiplied with every turn of the cards.

Many of the women who had been watching the players at the other tables came to stand behind him, and they gave little screams of delight every time he won.

There were only about fifty guests of the Grand Duke Boris present, but four gambling-tables were laid out in the elegant Salon which opened onto the garden of the Villa.

Standing high above the town, the Villa afforded a magnificent view over the harbour, the rock on which stood the Palace, and the sea itself.

However, no-one was concerned with anything but the playing of cards, and as the Duke won again a murmur of excitement ran through the spectators and even those who were playing against him.

The man who was sitting next to the Duke, and who had lost consistently all the evening, leant back in his chair with an air of exasperation, and the Duke heard a soft voice say:

"Unlucky at cards—lucky in love!"

It made him remember Imogen and he looked round to see if she was standing, as she usually did, at his side.

There was, however, no sign of her, and somewhere at the back of his mind he remembered seeing her move sometime ago through one of the long French windows into the garden.

He thought, although he was not sure, that the Grand Duke was with her, and for a moment as he waited to play there was a frown between his eyes.

The Grand Duke was noted for his fascination for women. It was not only because he was immensely rich and as generous as he could well afford to be, but also because he was in fact a very attractive man who had a charm which most women found irresistible.

The Duke remembered that Imogen had remarked as they drove up to the Villa how much she was looking forward to seeing their host and how delightful she found him.

The Duke was slightly piqued because he wished Imogen Moreton to think of no other man but himself, and particularly tonight.

As they steamed in his yacht from Marseilles to Monte Carlo he had decided that his bachelorhood was at an end and he would marry Lady Moreton, as everyone had been anticipating he would.

Her husband had been killed in the Boer War, but as she had married very young she was now only twenty-five and was at the height of her beauty.

The Duke had been pressed by his relations to find a wife, and it was in fact a miracle that he had reached the age of twenty-seven without being propelled up the aisle by some scheming Mama.

He had eluded all the bait that had been held out to him, all the tricks that might have ensnared him, and had determined at an early age that he would not be pressured in marrying anyone if he did not wish to do so.

He had inherited at the age of twenty-one and it had been impossible for him not to be conscious of his importance as one of the premier Dukes of Great Britain.

Women fawned on him, and because his name

was an old and respected one his company was sought
not only by those of his own generation but also by
Statesmen, Politicians, and men of distinction who
were older than himself.

He had been a friend of the Prince of Wales before he became King, and he was always a welcome
guest now at Buckingham Palace, as he had been at
Marlborough House.

The Duke had considered for a long time whether Imogen, who had been his mistress for over a year,
was the type of wife he wanted.

He admired her beauty, they had the same interests, and were both *persona grata* in the same
society.

It was very important, the Duke told himself,
that they should agree on the ordinary things which
filled their days, besides which he found Imogen very
desirable.

There had been a large party of his friends
aboard the *Aphrodite* who had sailed with them from
London to Monte Carlo, but they had left today and
another party was arriving tomorrow.

This meant that tonight when they returned to
the yacht the Duke would have Imogen to himself,
and he had decided that that was when he would
tell her that she was to be his wife.

It was something, he was well aware, that she
wanted beyond all else, and he did not doubt for a
moment that she loved him as a man.

All the same, something cynical told him she
would not be so keen on marriage if his position was
a less eminent one.

But then, he asked himself, how could anyone,
man or woman, be considered in isolation from their
background and their environment?

It was impossible to ask: "Would you love me if
I were not a Duke?" or for a woman: "Would you
love me if I were not beautiful?"

What was important was that they both were

well-bred, and both came from families which appeared in the history books.

The Cinderella story was only for housemaids and school-girls who read novelettes and consequently imagined that a Prince Charming was waiting to fall down the chimney to make them his bride.

"We will deal well together," the Duke told himself, "and my mother and everyone else will be delighted."

He planned that one of the first people to be told when they returned home should be the King.

His Majesty liked Imogen because she was beautiful, and he had intimated on two or three occasions to the Duke what a suitable wife she would make him.

'I will speak to her tonight,' the Duke told himself as they drove towards the Grand Duke's Villa.

But now Imogen was missing and it struck the Duke as strange that she had not returned from the garden.

Impatiently he rose from the table.

"Surely you are not giving up?" the man next to him exclaimed. "Not in the middle of a winning streak?"

The Duke did not answer, but leaving his money on the table walked across the Salon and out into the garden.

He was not in the least concerned that his behaviour might seem odd or that people would discuss it. They always discussed everything he did anyway, and if he wished to stop gambling that was his business and no-one else's.

The garden of the Grand Duke's Villa was filled with flowers and was extremely beautiful. It was actually one of the famous gardens of the Côte d'Azur.

This was due not so much to the money which the Grand Duke had spent on it as to the care and love given it by an old lady who had created it during the last years of her life.

There was the fragrance of flowers and the soft tinkle of a cascade in the water-garden, the petals from the blossoms on the flowering trees dropping silently onto the velvet grass. But the Duke noticed none of this.

He was looking for the scarlet gown that Imogen was wearing, which matched the necklace of rubies and diamonds he had given her before they had left England.

The garden was a complication of arbours, twisting paths, flowering bushes, and comfortable seats on which one could sit and look at the breathtaking view.

The Duke strode on. The place seemed to be deserted—then suddenly he saw her.

There was no mistaking the colour of her gown silhouetted against the white pillars of a small Grecian temple situated at the end of a grass walk bordered by flowers.

She was standing in a manner which the Duke knew very well, which drew attention to the sensuous lines of her figure and the beauty of her long, swan-like neck.

At the sight of her the Duke paused, and now as he watched her he saw the Grand Duke put his arms round her waist and pull her close to him.

She did not resist; in, fact she lifted her mouth eagerly to his, and as he kissed her lips her bare arm went round his neck to draw him even closer.

It was the classical, symbolic stance of a man and woman in love, and the scowl on the Duke's face deepened. Then, after he had stared at the passionately entwined pair, he walked away.

He did not return to the Villa but moved through the garden until he came to a gate which led to the road in front of it.

Drawn up in a long line were the carriages and horses of the guests, and it took him only a few seconds to locate his own carriage.

His servants looked surprised to see him. It was early and they had resigned themselves to a long wait—perhaps, as was usual in Monte Carlo, until dawn broke.

The footman opened the door and the Duke stepped into his carriage.

"The yacht!" he ordered.

The horses started off down the twisting road which descended sharply towards the harbour.

Inside the carriage, the Duke sat back, still frowning, and looking, although there was no-one to notice, extremely formidable.

Those who had heard him speak in the House of Lords knew that he was not only intelligent but could when aroused on a subject be both aggressive and determined.

It was in fact entirely due to him that several Bills that the Lords had meant to throw out had been passed, and the Prime Minister had thanked him gratefully for his assistance.

Those who served the Duke found him a just and generous master, but if he thought he was being cheated or that anyone in his employment was negligent or disloyal, he could be completely ruthless.

As the carriage reached the yacht, which was tied up to the quay along with a number of others, the Duke stepped out.

"I shall not require you again tonight," he said to the footman and walked off.

There was a Petty Officer on deck, and like the coachman he looked surprised to see the Duke returning so early.

"Good-evening, Your Gr—" he began, only to be interrupted as the Duke said curtly:

"Tell Captain Barnett to put to sea immediately!"

"Immediately, Your Grace?"

"That is what I said!"

"I will inform the Captain, Your Grace."

The Duke, still with a scowl on his face and an almost disinterested air, walked to the bow to watch as the sailors came hurrying on deck.

He imagined that some of them might have been

asleep, but his crew was quite used to his making decisions which changed their course or arriving on board without any warning.

It was the Duke's most explicit instruction that his yacht should always be ready to leave without any previous notification.

He knew now that Captain Barnett would not be surprised at being told to leave Monte Carlo and would be only awaiting orders as to where they were to head.

The Duke did not expect any questions, but they came nevertheless from his valet, a man called Dalton, who had been with him ever since a boy.

He had been chosen for the promotion by his father because he was a sensible man in whom he had every confidence.

"Excuse me, Your Grace," Dalton said at the Duke's elbow. "I wondered if Your Grace knows that Her Ladyship's not aboard?"

"I am aware of that."

The reply was uncompromising, but the valet persisted:

"Her Ladyship's clothes are still here, Your Grace."

"I am aware of that too!"

The valet bowed and departed. The Duke's lips were set in a grim line as he looked up over the town in the direction of the Grand Duke's Villa.

It would come as a shock to Imogen, he was well aware, that he had left the party without informing her of his intentions.

It would be an even greater shock when she found that he had sailed taking with him not only her clothes but also her jewellery, by which she set so much store.

'The Grand Duke can provide her with more,' the Duke thought savagely.

Then he told himself that he had had a lucky escape.

It was bad enough that the woman who professed to love him "as she had never loved a man before" should philander with such a notorious "lady-killer" as the Grand Duke, but it would have been far worse had she already become his wife.

He thought now that he would have been a fool to think that anyone who had been acclaimed and fêted as Imogen had been would ever want to settle down and be faithful to one man.

It was of course a blow to his pride and his self-conceit, and he acknowledged it as such.

He had grown monotonously accustomed to having any woman in whom he was even faintly interested, and a great many in whom he was not, falling ecstatically into his arms.

It was therefore quite a shock to realise that, as his Nanny would have put it, he was "not the only pebble on the beach."

There was a cynical smile on his lips as he felt the yacht moving slowly across the harbour and out into the Mediterranean.

Now there was a faint breeze, which he welcomed, and as he was deciding where he would tell his Captain to take him, he suddenly thought it was rather exhilarating to be alone.

It was a long time since he had not been surrounded by laughing, chattering people.

Templecombe House in London was always filled not only with his friends but also with large numbers of relations who thought it their right to stay there whenever they came to London from the country.

And Combe, in Buckinghamshire, was far too large for it not to seem imperative to fill the innumerable bed-rooms with innumerable guests and to augment the house-parties with his neighbours, all of whom expected to be invited whenever he was in residence.

Now he was alone and he thought that it was a desirable condition that he would enjoy to the full.

There were books to read and he would have a chance to think about himself and his future.

The yacht was far enough away from Monte

Carlo for the Duke to look back at the glittering lights which were concentrated round the Casino and climbed the hill behind it.

It was very beautiful but he knew that those who visited the Principality seldom raised their eyes from the tables and many in fact never rose from their beds until the glory of the day had passed and they could spend another night in the gambling-rooms.

'It has a false allure—as false as Imogen's,' the Duke thought.

Even as he recalled her, he told himself that the sooner he erased her completely from his mind, the better.

He did not want to remember his disgust and anger at her behaviour; he just wished to forget.

From the time he was a small boy he would never acknowledge when he was beaten, and would force himself to forget any humiliation he had suffered at school.

It was a sense of pride, ingrained in him by a long line of illustrious ancestors, which told him that he should not allow other people to encroach on him unless they were of importance to his happiness.

It was an idea put into his head by his father, who had once told him how Mr. Gladstone had written down the names of his enemies and shut the list in a locked drawer.

Years later he had taken it out and found that in nearly every instance he could not remember what that person had said or done, or why he had thought of them as enemies.

The story had impressed the Duke and it was something that he had tried to do all his life.

"Never give your enemies the importance of thinking of them," was one of his favourite sayings, and now he told himself that he had no intention, if he could help it, of ever giving Imogen another thought.

He would tell Dalton to pack up her clothes and her jewels and have them put in the hold. When they reached London, his secretary would see that they were delivered to her house and that would be the end.

It had been an enjoyable association, he thought. There was no denying that, and he had in fact begun to believe that Imogen was different from other women.

He thought love meant something in her life that did not resemble the shallow flattery that was so much part of the social life which centred round the King.

When Edward was Prince of Wales, the beauties he had fancied had been gossipped about from one end of England to the other.

There was not a man in the street who did not know of his infatuation for Lily Langtry, for the Countess of Warwick, and for half-a-dozen other lovely women.

The Duke had always admired the impeccable way the Danish-born Queen Alexandra behaved.

She never veered in her loyalty and devotion to her husband or in public showed any sign that she was upset or irritated by his constant infidelity.

The Duke supposed that, in a way, he had always fancied that his wife would behave in the same manner, but now he knew that where Imogen was concerned it was impossible.

She was too conscious of her beauty, too anxious to be admired, too weak to ignore the admiration of another man, even if his reputation was as infamous as that of the Grand Duke.

The Duke had a vision of himself moving down the years towards old age, wondering if his wife was unfaithful to him, always having his suspicions aroused and always being afraid to trust her.

"If that is what lies ahead," he told himself, "then damn all women! I shall never marry!"

His thoughts were not happy ones and he decided to go to the Saloon and have a drink.

He knew there would be an open bottle of cham-

Barbara Cartland

pagne waiting for him and beside it some wafer-thin sandwiches of *pâté de foie gras,* prepared just in case anyone would feel hungry when they returned on board.

Then as he turned to walk along the deck he heard someone speaking loudly on the bridge in a tone which told him that something was amiss.

Curious, it took him only a moment to stand beside the Captain, who had a telescope to his eye.

"What is it?" he asked.

"I am not sure, Your Grace. The look-out spotted what seems to be a body. It is something white—by Jove, it *is* a body!"

"Let me look."

The Captain handed the Duke the telescope and he steadied it in the experienced manner of a man who is used to stalking his own stags.

There was no doubt that there was something in the water, and as the Captain had said it was white. Then he was certain he could distinguish a face.

"You had better lower a boat and see if the person is alive," he said.

As he spoke, he thought it would be a suicide victim who had lost all his money at the tables.

It was the sort of tale that was always being repeated and rerepeated about Monte Carlo, although he had been told that in fact the majority of such stories were untrue.

The yacht hove-to and the sailors let down one of the boats.

At the last moment the Duke decided that he would go with those who were manning it.

He thought it would be wise for him to be there in case the body had been in the water for a long time, in which case it would not only be unnecessary but also extremely unpleasant to bring it on board.

He had seen men who had drowned, and their swollen faces and decomposing bodies were enough

66

to turn the stomach of the strongest and toughest old salt.

The Captain had brought the yacht to about a hundred yards from where the body was floating, and as the crew rowed towards it, the Duke bent forward, peering into the darkness.

There was no moon that night, but the stars were glowing brilliantly overhead. Nevertheless, it was hard to see clearly until they were right beside whatever it was on the surface of the water.

Then, to his astonishment, the Duke saw that the body was that of a child or a very young woman, wearing a white gown and floating on the surface of the sea.

Her arms were outstretched on either side of her, her head thrown back, her hair in the water, and the Duke knew that she was not only alive but also a very experienced swimmer to be able to float so effortlessly.

The boat drew nearer and still nearer, then the men nearest to the body lifted their oars and looked to the Duke for instructions.

"Catch hold of her hand," he said to the man at the bow.

The sound of his voice must have aroused the woman, for her eyes opened and she gave a scream.

Then as she saw the boat and the men in it peering down at her, she turned and tried to swim away.

She was, however, too late, for the sailor on the Duke's instructions had caught hold of her hand.

"Let ... me ... go! Let ... me ... go! I want ... to ... die!"

She struggled desperately, and taking the man who held her by surprise, she was free of him.

There was a struggle, or perhaps because she was so weak she sank slipping down beneath the water, and for a moment the Duke thought they had lost her.

But she came up again and this time the boat had swung so that the Duke was nearest to her. He

reached out and seized hold of her arm, managing
to get his hand on her shoulder.

She spluttered and would have protested, then
suddenly she collapsed, and it was only because the
Duke was so strong that he was able to hold her.

Slight though she was, as dead weight in the
water it was quite hard to pull her up into the boat.

When the Duke had managed it, with the
help of the sailor closest to him, he realised that her
legs were bare and she was clad only in a nightgown.

It clung tightly to her body, and because she was
so small and slight the Duke realised that while at a
distance it had been easy to mistake her for a child,
she was undoubtedly a young woman.

They reached the yacht and as the stairway had
been let down at the side it was easy for the Duke
to carry her in his arms up onto the deck.

The whole crew, including the Captain and
Dalton, seemed to be waiting for them, and without
wasting time in talking the Duke went below, followed hurriedly by Dalton.

The woman was entirely unconscious and the
Duke even wondered if she was dead as he carried
her into one of the empty cabins.

Hastily Dalton laid a number of thick Turkish
towels down on the floor and he laid her down on
them aware that his shirt-front and his trousers were
wet.

"I'll manage, Your Grace," Dalton said.

"Get some brandy," the Duke ordered, "and
more towels!"

"Very good, Your Grace."

The Duke looked down at the woman he had
rescued, and in the bright lights of the cabin he
realised that he had been right in thinking that what
she was wearing was a nightgown.

But it was in fact an elaborate and very expensive one. The lace that trimmed it was real and he
saw that on her finger she wore a wedding-ring. He
wondered if she had been thrown from a yacht by

some murderously inclined husband, but it seemed more likely because of her cry that she wished to die, that she had tried to commit suicide.

It seemed inconceivable that she had swum so far from the shore. Very few women of the Duke's acquaintance could swim at all.

But, wherever she had come from, she was certainly a mystery. He noticed too that she was not only very young but very pretty, even with her hair wet and lank against her white cheeks.

Divesting himself of his evening-coat, which was too close-fitting for such athletic exertions, the Duke picked up a towel, then decided that the first thing he must do was to remove the soaked nightgown of the woman he had saved.

It fastened at the front, and he undid several pearl-shaped buttons, then, modestly covering the lower half of her body with a towel, he pulled it up.

There was no doubt, he thought, that she was beautifully made. Her body was exquisite and she might have been the young Aphrodite rising from the waves.

'I am being poetical,' the Duke told himself almost angrily.

He had been hating all women until this happened. Now he could not help feeling a rising curiosity about this woman who had come into his life so unexpectedly.

He pulled the wet nightgown up to Salena's head and with an arm under her shoulders raised her a little so that he could remove it altogether. As he did so, he found that it was torn from the yoke. Then he saw her back.

He stared, incredulous, finding it hard to believe that his eyes were not deceiving him. This was certainly an explanation of her having jumped overboard.

The Prince's whip had seared Salena's body in a criss-cross pattern of weals breaking the flesh in several places so that they were bleeding.

The Duke pulled away the wet nightgown, then as he heard Dalton returning he laid Salena down and hurriedly covered her with another towel.

"Here's the brandy, Your Grace," Dalton said, handing him a glass, "and two more towels. I'll fetch some others right away."

"Do that."

Very gently the Duke rubbed Salena's hair with one of the towels which Dalton had brought him.

He found that it was not loose, as he had first thought, but there were hair-pins caught in it, as if it had been arranged and not free when she had entered the water.

This was another thing to puzzle him, and as her hair became drier under his ministrations he saw that she was very fair, and he wondered what colour her eyes were.

"Blue, I suppose," he told himself.

She was still unconscious when Dalton returned, and the Duke said:

"I think it would be wise to get this young woman into bed before we try to bring her round."

"A good idea, Your Grace."

"I suggest you spread one of the large bath-towels on the bed and fetch some hot-water bottles. She is very cold."

"I'll do that, Your Grace."

The valet pulled back the bed-clothes and spread a Turkish towel on the bottom sheet and a smaller towel over the pillow.

"There's another one handy with which you can cover her, Your Grace. I'll not be long with the hot-water bottles."

He hurried busily away from the cabin, and the Duke waited until he was gone before he lifted Salena in his arms.

He had the idea that her nakedness should not be exposed to anyone but himself and as he carried her towards the bed he found how light she was.

"How could any man beat anything so exquisite?" he asked.

Then he wondered if in fact her husband had caught her out in an act of infidelity.

Even so, to have punished her so cruelly and so brutally was something no decent man would have done.

The Duke laid Salena down on the bed, covered her with the extra towel, then pulled on top of it the sheets and blankets.

Her cheeks were almost as pale as the linen and he wondered if she would be happier if he left her. Then he knew it would be a mistake to let her drift into what might prove to be a coma.

He slipped his arm under her head and, lifting her, said firmly:

"Wake up! Wake up and drink this!"

He had the feeling, although he could not be sure, that she was fighting to remain oblivious to everything that was happening.

He was sure he was right in his supposition when her eye-lids flickered. Then, as she felt the glass against her lips, she tried to turn her head to one side.

"Drink!" the Duke said commandingly.

As if she was too weak to disobey him, she swallowed the drops of brandy he tipped between her lips.

She held her breath, and he thought she was defying him. Then he forced a little more of the brandy into her mouth, as she struggled to move her arms.

"Lie still and drink!" the Duke said.

"N-no . . . !"

It was a very weak sound but somehow she managed to say it.

He still held the glass to her mouth, and finally, when she had taken a few more sips of brandy and swallowed them almost despite herself, her eyes opened.

71

She stared at the Duke with an expression of horror, and because his arm was round her he felt her whole body go tense and knew it was with fear.

"It is all right," he said soothingly. "You are quite safe."

"N-no ... !" she managed to say again. "No ... no! Let me ... die!"

"It is too late for that," he said quietly.

Gently he put her head back on the pillow.

She was still staring at him with an expression of abject terror in her eyes. Yet he was not certain whether she was seeing him or something which had frightened her before she had entered the water.

"You are quite safe," he repeated. "And now you must tell me where you have come from and where you would like me to take you."

He thought she did not understand what he was saying, and when she did not speak he asked:

"Suppose we start by you telling me who you are? What is your name?"

"S ... Sal ... en ... a."

She spoke the word very slowly, with a pause between each syllable.

"And your other name?"

She gave a little scream that was so small and so weak that it was like the cry of a new-born kitten.

She shut her eyes and lay back, holding her breath as if trying to force herself back into unconsciousness, and the Duke saw that she was trembling.

He wondered how he should deal with someone in such a state.

He had not realised that it was possible for a woman to look so frightened, so abjectly terrified.

It was not surprising considering the way she had been treated, and yet he thought that perhaps, unless he was being overly imaginative, it was not only the beating that had scared her but something else.

He had not spoken or moved, and as if she was

curious to see whether he had left, Salena opened her eyes.

She saw him, and once again appeared to shrink away, to sink into the bed, trying to disappear.

"No-one will hurt you," the Duke said quietly. "There is nothing here to make you afraid."

He was not certain whether she understood. There was only the expression of horror on her face, and the pupils of her eyes seemed so dilated that they were black.

Dalton appeared with two hot-water bottles.

"I'll slip one in by the young lady's feet, Your Grace," he said, handing the other one to the Duke.

Very gently the Duke raised the sheets to put the bottle beside Salena but on top of the towel which covered her.

"You will feel warmer with this," he said. "It must have been very cold in the sea."

He noticed that she winced and shrank away from him when he placed the bottle beside her.

'Whatever happened to her,' he thought, 'it has certainly given her a fear of men.'

It was an interesting thought, and he looked at her contemplatively, noting the flower-like, childish face, the huge eyes set far apart, and the perfect curve of her trembling little mouth.

'Whoever the man was who beat her,' the Duke thought, 'he is a swine! It would be a pleasure to give him a taste of his own medicine!'

Dalton was picking up the wet towels that had been left on the floor and the sodden nightgown.

He walked to the door before he stopped to say:

"Do you think, Your Grace, I might get the young lady one of Her Ladyship's nightgowns? It'll be too big, but I'm sure she'd feel more comfortable in it."

"That is a good idea, Dalton," the Duke replied. "But I will not put it on her at the moment but will merely leave it here on the bed. Also bring a dressing-gown and a pair of slippers."

He felt somewhat cynically that he had no compunction about using Imogen's wardrobe, seeing that he had paid for most of it.

Salena had half-shut her eyes but the Duke was sure she was watching him.

It was as if he were a ferocious animal which might attack her and she was too afraid not to keep her eyes on him in case she was taken by surprise.

He walked across the cabin so as to be as far from her as possible. Then he said quietly:

"You must tell me what you want to do. My yacht hove-to to rescue you, but I must now instruct my Captain where to go."

He spoke slowly, as if to a child, but her eyes were on his face and he had the feeling that she understood exactly what he was saying.

After a moment he asked:

"Do you wish to return to Monte Carlo?"

"No! No!"

There was no doubt of the terror in her voice.

"Then where shall we go?"

"Away ..."

He could hardly hear the word.

"Very well then," the Duke said. "We will go away from Monte Carlo, and as you apparently have no preference, I will take you with me to Tangier where I have a Villa. It will take us a few days to get there and perhaps by then you will be able to tell me a little more about yourself."

Salena did not reply and he walked towards the door.

"Try to sleep," he said. "Everything will seem better in the morning."

She did not answer but she was watching him, and as he went from the room he turned out the lights in the cabin, with the exception of the one by the bed.

He was moving into his own cabin, which was next door, to take off his damp clothes, when an idea struck him.

74

Once she recovered her senses, this girl who had been so anxious to die might easily attempt to drown herself again.

In her present state of weakness, it would not be difficult.

The Duke stepped backwards and very softly shot home the bolt, one of which was on the outside of each of the doors on his yacht.

They had been fitted as a precaution against thieves and had a special mechanism which made them impossible to open by those who were not aware of it.

When they were in harbour, although there was always someone on watch, the Duke had learnt with his other yachts that it was easy for an experienced thief to climb aboard and help himself to anything that was available.

These bolts, which he had invented himself, made this almost impossible.

There were all sorts of new gadgets he had incorporated in his new yacht which had been manufactured to his own specifications.

He had enjoyed building the *Aphrodite* and he had been pleased by the appreciation of his friends when on reaching Marseilles they had first seen her.

He remembered now that he had another party, coming from London, which would arrive in Monte Carlo tomorrow. They would certainly think it extraordinary that he was not there to greet them.

He decided that the only recompense he could make was to send a wireless message first thing in the morning telling them in his unavoidable absence to be his guests at the Hôtel de Paris.

They were all people who knew the ways of the world, he thought, and it would not be long before they discovered the reason why he had left and why Imogen had not accompanied him.

"Let them gossip!" he exclaimed savagely.

It suddenly occurred to him that if they knew what was happening at this moment aboard the

Aphrodite it would give them an even tastier tit-bit of scandal to chatter about.

The idea of his rescuing a half-naked, brutally beaten young woman from the sea would appeal to their imagination and undoubtedly keep them speculating until they discovered the identity of the unexpected passenger.

'I am sure I have never seen her before,' the Duke thought.

If he had seen anyone so young and so lovely in Monte Carlo he would have been bound to notice her.

Later, when the Duke returned to bed, he found it impossible not to keep going over in his mind the few clues that he had about the young woman sleeping in the next cabin.

Obviously she was not poverty-stricken—he could tell that by the expensive nightgown she had been wearing. She wore a wedding-ring, but because she was so young she could not have been married very long.

She was beautiful, and yet, and perhaps because of it, some man had frightened her until she was terror-stricken by the whole male sex.

"We certainly have one thing in common," the Duke told himself. "I am hating women at the moment, and she is hating men. Her conversation, if I can persuade her to speak, should certainly be informative."

❋   ❋   ❋

It was Dalton who the next day gave the Duke the information that his unknown passenger was awake.

"I took the young lady a cup of tea, Your Grace," Dalton said, "and asked her what she'd like for breakfast. But she seemed almost as frightened, Your Grace, as she were last night."

"Did she say anything to you?" the Duke enquired.

He was having his own breakfast in the Dining-Saloon and finding after the drama of the night before that he was in fact surprisingly hungry.

"She said: 'Anything!' Your Grace. Just like that —'Anything,' and she sort of shivered when she spoke. I suppose it must be the shock of having fallen into the water."

"Yes, I expect that is what it is," the Duke said casually. "Take the lady some breakfast, Dalton, and then come back. I want to speak to you."

"Very good, Your Grace."

When Dalton returned, the Duke was finishing his second cup of coffee, and as the valet stood waiting by the table he said:

"We will have to use our ingenuity, Dalton, in finding the young lady something to wear."

"I've thought of that, Your Grace."

"You have?"

"Well, thinking how small the lady is, Your Grace, I realised it would be impossible, unless they was altered, for her to wear anything belonging to Her Ladyship."

"Exactly," the Duke agreed. "That is what I thought myself!"

"But I remembers, Your Grace," Dalton went on, "that the Captain's got a daughter aged fourteen and I knows that he bought her two dresses when he was in Marseilles, pretty and French they are, and just about the right size, I should say."

"That is very helpful of you, Dalton," the Duke approved. "Suggest to the young lady that when she is well enough to use them, she should try them on. Any other garments she may require you may give her from Lady Moreton's cabin."

"Thank you, Your Grace."

"And tell the Captain that of course I will reimburse him, and I am certain he can find something equally suitable for his daughter in Tangier or when we return to Marseilles."

"I'll tell the Captain, Your Grace."

The Duke also remembered to thank the Captain himself when he went up to the bridge.

"I was thinking, Your Grace," Captain Barnett said, "that we were fortunate in finding the young lady. I was moving away from the shore, and another second or so and we'd not have seen her."

"She was obviously not meant to die, Captain," the Duke replied.

"Seems strange that she should want to," Captain Barnett remarked.

The Duke, remembering the weals on Salena's back, thought he knew of one good reason why she had no wish to cling to life, but he had no intention of imparting to the Captain, or to anyone else, what he had seen.

When he went to the Saloon before luncheon he found to his surprise that Salena was there waiting for him.

He did not miss the fact that as he entered the room she started and made a movement as if she would run away.

But as he was standing in the doorway and there was no other way out, she seemed to shrink and become even smaller than she was already.

As if her legs would no longer carry her, she sat down on the corner of one of the sofas.

"Good-morning, Salena," the Duke said. "I hope you are feeling better. May I say that is a very becoming gown you are wearing?"

It was in fact a very attractive dress for a teenage girl.

Of white, trimmed with broderie anglaise, it was very simple and not expensive, but it had a French style about it that was unmistakable.

"Th-thank you ... for ... all your ... kindness," Salena said in a hesitating little voice, "b-but I ... wanted to ... die .... It was ... only ..."

She stopped, and after a moment the Duke prompted:

78

"Only what?"

"As I can ... swim ... I found it ... difficult to ... make myself ... sink."

Salena had learnt to swim first at Bath in the famous Roman Baths when she had gone with her mother one winter after Lady Cardenham had been ill with a touch of pneumonia.

Salena had been very young at the time and her father had laughed at the manner in which she had taken to the water. "Like a small tadpole!" he had said.

After that she had always bathed with her cousins when she stayed in her grandfather's house in the country.

Lady Cardenham's father lived in a large mansion with a lake in the park.

His grandchildren, who with the exception of Salena were all boys, had during the summer raced one another across the lake, upset their canoes on purpose, and practised life-saving in case they should ever be in a wreck at sea.

Salena had adored every moment of it, and although it had been impossible to swim these last two years when she had been at school, in France she had always managed the precious summers, even while as she grew older her mother disapproved of what was called "mixed bathing."

When she had swum away from the Prince's Villa last night she had intended to swim on and on until she was too tired to go any farther.

Then she would just drop like a stone to the bottom of the ocean.

That would be the end. No-one would ever find her again and there would be no accusations about the crime she had committed, nor would she have to face trial, imprisonment, or, perhaps, death.

She could not bear to think of the Prince crying out that she had killed him as the blood seeped onto the bed from the knife-wound in his stomach.

She did not want to remember, she did not want

even to think of it, but she knew that her whole body was tense with fear.

Even to look at the Duke, because he was a man, made her feel a terror rising inside her as it had done when the Prince had whipped her.

The Duke sat down in a chair some way from Salena.

"Last night," he said, "you told me your name—at least half of it—but I think now we should introduce ourselves formally. I am the Duke of Templecombe!"

Suddenly there was a look in Salena's eyes which told him she knew the name.

"You have heard of me?" he asked.

"Then . . . this is . . . the *Aphrodite?*"

"Yes, that is the name of my yacht."

"It is . . . very beautiful."

She was thinking how lovely it had looked and how excited she had been while driving along the road with her father.

She had not known then, had not realised, what was waiting for her, and she felt herself tremble again as she thought of the Prince.

The Duke was watching the expressions that changed and altered her face.

He had never before known a woman who had such expressive eyes, or who seemed so small and pathetic.

He was perceptive enough to realise that she was tortured by her thoughts, and he knew that if he was to gain her confidence he must not say anything to upset her.

"I hope you like my yacht," he said in a casual manner. "It is a new acquisition. I designed it myself and I am very proud of it. It has a lot of features that no other vessel of its kind has ever had. When you are feeling better I will show them to you."

The terror seemed to slip away from Salena's eyes and after a moment she asked:

"W-we are not going back to . . . Monte Carlo?"

"You said you had no wish to go there," the Duke

80

replied, "and so I am taking you with me to Tangier.
I told you so last night, but I expect you were too upset to understand."

"I ... I thought you ... said that ... but I was
afraid I had ... misunderstood you."

"We are going to Tangier," the Duke affirmed. "I
have a Villa there, which, as it happens, I have not
visited for some time. I hope you will find it as beautiful as the *Aphrodite*."

"I ... have no ... money," Salena said.

"As you are my guest, that is of no particular importance," the Duke answered. "If when we reach
Tangier you wish to go anywhere else, I can always
lend you whatever money you need."

He paused before he added quietly:

"Perhaps you would wish to get in touch with
your family?"

"No! No!"

The cry he had heard before was on Salena's lips
and once again she seemed to shake with fear.

She thought wildly to herself that her father
would never forgive her for her behaviour to the
Prince, and he must believe her dead.

She only hoped he would be able to keep the
money which the Prince had already given him.
Then she remembered that there could be no argu-
ment about that, because the Prince, being dead,
could not claim it back.

'Papa will be all right,' she told herself, 'but he
must never know that I am alive.'

It suddenly struck her that it would be impossible to live if she had no money and nowhere to go.

Without meaning to, she looked piteously at the
Duke and clasped her hands together as if she were
a child begging his assistance.

"I see you are still feeling upset," he said, "so,
suppose I ask no more questions and you just try to
enjoy yourself? After all, it is a lovely day and we
are alone in the Mediterranean and no-one knows we
are here."

He thought he saw a light in her eyes, and he went on:

"I have often thought myself what fun it would be to disappear and start life again. It would be like beginning a new book about one's self."

He saw that he was on the right track, so he went on:

"If anyone is aware that you fell into the sea and is looking for you, he will be disappointed. And let me tell you, no-one in Monte Carlo has any idea where I have gone, so they are not likely to connect us with each other."

He smiled before he added:

"You are free, free of everything, even the things which are alarming you. Nobody knows where you are or what you have done!"

"C-can that ... really be ... true?" Salena asked.

"I am sure of it," the Duke replied.

"But ... God ... knows ... !"

The words were spoken almost beneath her breath, but the Duke heard them.

"Yes, God knows," he answered, "but we have always been told He is merciful and very understanding, and so I assure *you*, Salena, you need not be frightened of Him."

Even as he spoke, he thought to himself that it was a most extraordinary and unusual way for him to be talking.

But as he saw the tension leave Salena and the calmer manner in which she looked at him, he knew that he had said the right thing.

'Now what can this child possibly have done,' he asked himself, 'to make her afraid of the retribution of God as well as of man?'

Chapter Four

The steward came in to announce that luncheon was ready, and the Duke saw Salena start as he entered the Saloon and stare at him wildly as if for a moment she had expected someone else.

Pretending not to notice, he rose, saying:

"As it is such a warm day, I thought we would have our meal on deck."

He led the way and Salena followed him to where there were two large wicker chairs filled with soft cushions.

They had foot-rests, and because she realised it was expected of her she lowered herself carefully onto the cushions.

The Duke saw her wince and knew it was from the pain in her back. He was quite sure that by now it was extremely painful, for the weals would have stiffened and scabs would be forming over the places which had bled.

When she was in the chair Salena looked at him almost piteously, as if she was afraid of what would happen next.

The Duke covered her with a warm rug, then the steward fitted what appeared to be a tabletop with iron supports into the sides of the chair.

She looked down at it wonderingly, and as the Duke sat down in a similar chair beside her he said:

"This is an invention of my own. I thought it

83

would be nice to be outside if I was alone or had only one person to eat with me."

He smiled as he added:

"You are in fact christening my idea, for this is the first time I have seen it in action."

"It is very ... clever of ... you," Salena said.

The steward placed another tray, already laid with a white cloth, glasses, knives, and forks on top of the improvised table.

Other stewards brought out a number of delicious dishes, and it was, Salena thought, an original and comfortable way of eating.

There was an awning over their heads, the sea was very blue but calm, and there was only the soft throb of the engines and the cry of the seagulls.

It was very different, she thought, from the noisy luncheon-parties which had taken place in the Villa, with the Prince's guests talking either in French or in Russian.

Their voices had seemed to grow louder as their crystal glasses were filled and refilled with different wines.

"I am going to persuade you to have a small glass of champagne," said the Duke at her side. "I feel it will bring the colour back to your cheeks and help you to feel happy again."

Salena wanted to say that that would be impossible, but she thought it would sound rude and so when the champagne was poured out she took a little sip.

The Duke, however, was looking out to sea.

"I think there are some porpoises over there," he said. "I hope they come nearer to the yacht. I always find their antics amusing to watch."

"Porpoises?" Salena exclaimed. "I have heard about them, but I have never seen one."

"They are quite frequently to be found in the Mediterranean," the Duke replied.

"One ... of the ... nuns at the ... Convent," she said in a hesitating little voice, "said that where she

... came from in the South of Italy, the peasants ... believed that when a sailor was ... d-drowned at ... sea, his soul became a ... porpoise. ..."

Her voice died away, and the Duke was sure that she was thinking that this was what might have happened to her soul if she had drowned as she had intended.

The Duke said:

"Many primitive people who live by the sea have that belief. In the Orkneys and in the Shetland Islands, for instance, the inhabitants think that the souls of fishermen become seals, which is why they will never kill one."

To himself he thought he had another clue to the puzzle of Salena. She had been at a Convent.

He felt as if he were an archaeologist discovering traces of a bygone civilisation, or an ornithologist in pursuit of some unknown species of bird.

He had never before in the whole of his life been alone with a woman who was not interested in him as a man, or was so afraid that she winced and shrank away from him when he approached her.

It was a new experience and it interested him; he found himself growing increasingly curious about Salena.

He told himself that sooner or later he would discover what had upset her and that he would find out who she was.

Meanwhile, he talked quietly of impersonal things as they ate. Then, as he finished the last course, he turned to say something to Salena and saw that she had fallen asleep.

He realised it was a sleep of complete exhaustion and knew that what she had suffered yesterday would have taken its toll of any man, let alone a weak woman.

The steward approached and the Duke put his finger to his lips to ensure silence. The man lifted the tray from in front of Salena and walked silently away with it.

Another steward removed the Duke's tray and offered him brandy, which he refused. Then there was nothing to disturb Salena and the Duke looked at her at his leisure.

Her face was turned towards him and her cheek was buried against a soft blue cushion which accentuated her pallor and also the fairness of her hair.

With her eyes closed she looked very young and very vulnerable. Then as she stirred she moved her hand, and the Duke saw that she no longer wore her wedding-ring. He had noticed it last night, so there was no doubt that it had been on her finger.

He wondered if she had torn it off in disgust for what she had suffered and thrown it through the port-hole, or whether she hoped to deceive him by pretending that she was not married.

Then, looking at her, he told himself it would be impossible for her to deceive anyone.

There was something so obviously and transparently pure and good about her that it was unthinkable to believe that she was not as innocent as she appeared.

And yet, he asked himself, who was he to judge?

He had been deceived by women before, and however innocent Salena might seem, it was obvious that a man had beaten her, and doubtless it was the man who had paid for the expensive nightgown she had been wearing.

It was an extraordinary situation, he thought, in which to find himself. It took him a great deal of thought to decide how best he could allay Salena's fears and what he should do with her in the future.

She was like a wild animal, he thought, that had been trapped and ill-treated to the point where it was impossible for it to know who was a friend and who was foe.

He knew that somehow he must gain her trust before he could really help her.

She was sleeping so deeply that he knew for the moment at any rate her fears were forgotten.

He smiled as he thought that none of the people who were certainly gossipping about his precipitate departure from Monte Carlo would, in their wildest imaginings, guess what he was actually doing.

If Imogen, or any other woman on whom he had bestowed his favours in the past, was in Salena's place, she would be flirting with him, demanding his attention, and striving with every provocative wile to excite him.

He had the idea that if he showed even a semblance of interest in Salena it would terrify her even more than she was already.

"Perhaps," he told himself mockingly, "I have been over-rating my attractions in the past and this will prove a very salutary lesson to me."

It was an hour later when Salena awoke with a little jerk.

She looked towards the Duke and gasped.

"I . . . I am sorry . . . I fell . . . asleep," she said. "It was . . . rude of me."

"But it is understandable that you should be tired," the Duke replied. "I expected you to stay in bed today."

"Your valet . . . suggested it," Salena answered, "but I . . . I wanted to get up."

The Duke guessed that she was afraid of staying alone with only her thoughts, but aloud he said:

"On the *Aphrodite* you can do exactly what you wish to do."

She did not answer but looked out on the sunlit water, and he thought that one of the unusual things about her was that she was so unselfconscious.

Any other woman of his acquaintance having been asleep in his presence, would now have been tidying her hair, fussing about her complexion and even daringly, if one of the more sophisticated beauties, applying powder to repair the ravages of the wind and the sea-air.

But Salena just lay still, with her hands in her lap, and after a moment the Duke said:

"You have only told me your Christian name. It is a little difficult to know how the servants should address you. Should they say Miss or Madam?"

He saw the fingers of her hand lying on the rug tremble, then she said:

"I ... I ... am not ... married."

The Duke raised his eye-brows.

So that, he thought, was why she had thrown away her wedding-ring. But why had she needed it in the first place?

Surely she had not pretended to be some man's wife so that she could spend an illicit weekend or a holiday with him?

Such an idea was so alien to her appearance that he could not entertain it.

Then he said in an indifferent voice:

"Then I will tell the stewards that you are Miss Salena, unless you wish to tell me your surname?"

"I ... I have ... forgotten it."

Her eye-lashes flickered as she spoke and the Duke knew that this was not true.

It was so transparently false that he was quite sure that Salena not only found it difficult to lie but the thought of it was wrong, if not a sin.

Obviously, that would be part of her Convent upbringing.

"Have you been to Tangier before?" he asked.

"No ... never ..."

"I find it very attractive and the climate is perfect at this time of the year."

There was silence, and then suddenly in a frightened little voice Salena asked:

"It ... it does not ... belong to the ... French?"

There was no doubt that this idea terrified her, and he said soothingly:

"No, not at the moment, although the French are always wanting to occupy certain parts of Morocco."

"But not ... Tangier?"

"No, and it is very unlikely that they will be allowed by Germany or England to encroach farther in Northern Africa."

He spoke to allay her fears, but his brain was puzzling out why the idea of the French should be so terrifying.

Then he thought that perhaps either the man who had beaten her was French, or else she had broken a French law which might involve the Police.

It seemed impossible that this child—and it was difficult to think of her otherwise—would do anything that would involve her with the French authorities, but undoubtedly the fear was there.

After a moment the Duke said:

"I do not want to sound conceited, but I have a certain amount of influence both in my own country and abroad, and I think I can assure you confidently that while you are with me you will be safe from anything or anybody who might perturb you."

He thought he saw some light of hope in her eyes. Then she shook her head.

"You must . . . not be . . . involved in any way . . . because that might . . . harm your reputation."

The Duke looked at her in astonishment.

"My reputation?" he repeated.

"Pa—"

She bit back the word and said hastily, as if she thought he had not noticed:

"S-someone told me how . . . important you are."

'So she has a father,' the Duke thought, and wondered if in fact it was her father who had beaten her. But, if so, why the wedding-ring?

And what man, however bestial, would throw his own child into the sea after having maltreated her as Salena had been?

"If I am as important as you say I am," he said aloud, "it gives me the power to help other people when they are in trouble, and that is why I wish to help you, Salena."

"You are . . . very kind . . . but it would have been . . . better if you had let me . . . d-die."

"Better for you or better for me?" the Duke asked lightly.

"I . . . th-think for both of us," Salena answered seriously.

"Well, as far as I am concerned, I am very glad that I rescued you," the Duke said, "and I cannot help thinking it was fate that the *Aphrodite* was passing by at just that particular moment."

He knew Salena was listening, and he went on:

"My Captain said that a few seconds more and you would have been out of our sight. So you see, Salena, it really was fate—or perhaps, as you might say, the hand of God."

"It is . . . very wicked to try to take one's own . . . l-life," Salena said in a hesitating little voice, "b-but it . . . seemed to me there was . . . nothing else I could . . . do."

"That is what *you* thought, but obviously your Guardian Angel had other ideas," the Duke said.

Salena gave a little sigh.

"I ought to be very . . . grateful, but I do not . . . know what to do now."

"That is quite easy," the Duke answered. "Just enjoy a voyage on the *Aphrodite*. I can assure you that a number of people would be quite eager to be in your place."

"I know that," Salena said quickly, "and I am ashamed of . . . forcing myself . . . upon you."

"I think it was I who forced you to accept my hospitality," the Duke replied. "In fact, you were extremely reluctant to be my guest."

He thought there was a faint smile on her lips, and he went on:

"I have always imagined, again conceitedly, that people are eager to accept my invitations. It is quite a change, however, literally to kidnap someone so that I can enjoy their company."

"You are . . . being very kind," Salena said, "and I know I ought to . . . try to amuse you . . . and make you ... laugh ... but that is something I can never ... never do ... again."

Salena spoke almost passionately as she thought of the Prince and how her father had told her to be nice to him. She had tried, and the result was that he wanted her in a way which made her feel physically sick to remember.

Her face was very expressive and the Duke rose from his chair to walk to the railing.

"I am looking for porpoises," he said. "Do not move. I will tell you when I see them."

'He has been so kind to me,' Salena thought, 'and he must ... find me a dismal ... boring companion.'

She remembered the envy in her father's voice when, after the Duke had spoken to him in the Casino, he had told her who the Duke was.

He had appeared to be alone, but she was quite certain that there had been many lovely ladies, glittering with jewels, who were with him or were willing to talk to him.

When Dalton had brought her a number of exquisite lace underclothes such as *Madame* Yvette had provided for her at the Villa, she had looked at them in surprise.

"His Grace says you can borrow anything that you require," the valet explained hastily, "from one of his guests who has stayed behind in Monte Carlo."

"Will she not mind?" Salena had asked, knowing it was a relief to find that she had not to continue to be naked.

At the same time, she felt it was somehow wrong to use such beautiful garments which belonged to another woman.

"Her Ladyship won't know, and even if she does it isn't likely to trouble her," Dalton replied.

It was obvious to him that Lady Moreton had done something to make the Duke so angry that he had come aboard in a rage and left her behind in Monte Carlo.

Naturally, the crew were speculating about what had happened.

They had all been betting that the Duke would soon announce his engagement to Her Ladyship, and in fact the only person who had been sceptical about it was Dalton.

He had seen so many of the Duke's favourites come and go.

While undoubtedly Lady Moreton had lasted longer than the rest, there was something about her which made Dalton feel that she was not suitable for the master, whom he admired whole-heartedly.

No-one knew better than Dalton that His Grace had never really been deeply and completely in love.

He had been infatuated and at times even besotted with some alluring Socialite who had pursued him relentlessly and had captured him with the air of a Red Indian adding another scalp to his belt.

But somehow, even when the pursuer was certain of the prey, the Duke had always wriggled out of the trap at the last moment.

Certainly he had been extremely attached to Lady Moreton, and watching them together Dalton had at times thought that there would be a mistress at last in the Duke's magnificent houses.

But little things that Lady Moreton had said and done had made the valet think that she was too fond of herself to be whole-heartedly in love with the Duke, however fascinating he was to the majority of her sex.

Nevertheless, by the time they had reached Monte Carlo, Lady Moreton had felt very sure of how their association would end.

She had once said to Dalton in an unguarded moment when speaking of Combe House:

"I shall change that."

He had known that she was referring to when

she became the Duchess, and with difficulty he had prevented himself from replying:

"Never count your chickens, M'Lady, until they're hatched!"

"I must have sensed this would happen," Dalton had told himself the previous night, when the Duke came on board with a scowl on his face and the *Aphrodite* had sailed, leaving Lady Moreton behind.

He was an inquisitive little man and he found it exasperating to know that he would never learn exactly what had happened.

One thing, however, was quite certain: Lady Moreton would not become the Duchess of Templecombe, and as far as he was concerned that was a good thing.

He therefore pressed Imogen's most exotic and expensive garments on Salena.

He thought with regret that because she was so small and slight it would be impossible for her to wear any of the elaborate ball-gowns or the extremely expensive day-dresses which were hanging in Lady Moreton's wardrobe.

Her shoes were too big too, and only by stuffing a little cotton-wool into the toes of her bed-room slippers was Salena able to wear them under the cotton dress which had been bought by the Captain for his daughter.

This, unfortunately, was a little too long, so the slippers were hidden, and Dalton decided that when they reached Gibraltar he would ask the Duke if he could go ashore and find some things that would fit her.

He too was intrigued, and wondered what had made her so terrified and why she had been floating so far out at sea.

That she had tried to drown herself had of course been repeated by the sailors in the boat and had lost nothing in the telling.

'She's too young to have suffered so much,' Dalton thought savagely.

93

He tried to show Salena his sympathy by providing her with everything she wanted.

There was no sign of any porpoises, but a fresh wind sprang up and the Duke said to Salena:

"I think you should go below. After all you have been through, it would be very easy to catch a chill, and although Dalton would doubtless enjoy nursing you, I would have no-one to talk to at mealtimes."

"But you must have ... wanted to be ... alone," Salena said.

"I wanted to be free of noisy parties and people gossiping about each other," the Duke replied. "As you come into neither of those categories, may I say I am delighted to have you with me."

It was a very mild compliment and he was afraid she might be frightened by it, but she did not appear to be listening to him.

Although he did not know it, she was thinking once again of the parties in the Villa and how strange and incomprehensible the conversations had been to her.

The Prince must have banked on nobody speaking of his wife, and that was, she thought, because *Madame* Versonne apparently had such a proprietory hold over him.

It suddenly struck her for the first time that *Madame* Versonne had been the Prince's mistress.

Although she had realised that the Frenchwoman was very jealous of anyone else to whom he spoke, and especially to Salena, she had never queried that *Madame* Versonne's position was anything other than that of an ordinary guest.

His mistress!

It seemed horrifying that while having a mistress in Monte Carlo and a wife in Russia, the Prince had also wanted her and actually paid her father a large sum to possess her.

Salena wanted to cry out with the pain such thoughts aroused in her.

She loved her father—she had always loved him

—and it seemed incredible and degrading that he would stoop to selling her to obtain money.

Now she understood what he had meant when he kept saying: "If only there were time . . ." Time perhaps to find her a real husband, not a man who would just put on an act for her benefit.

Snatches of conversation, her father's insistence that he was a bad father and yet loved her, and the way everything had been done so quickly and secretly confronted her with the truth.

The knowledge that her father had connived with the Prince to deceive her, simply because they knew they dare not tell her the truth, was shaming.

The Duke had turned his back on the sea and was leaning against the railing facing her.

He had wondered why Salena had not replied to what he had said to her and now he saw the expression on her face.

It was as if she expressed her suffering without words, and he knew that whatever had happened had disgusted her to the point where she felt both degraded and humiliated.

'Whatever I can say will only make it worse,' he decided.

At the same time, his curosity deepened and he had to exert all his self-control not to question her, not almost to beg her to confide in him.

They went to the Saloon and Salena was looking so pale that the Duke suggested she should rest on her bed.

He thought she might protest, but she agreed, and he rang for Dalton to fill her hot-water bottles.

Alone in the Saloon, the Duke picked up a book that he had been looking forward to reading, but he found it almost impossible to concentrate on the pages.

All he could see was a flower-like face filled with two huge eyes that expressed an agony of suffering in a manner he had never seen before.

"What the devil can have happened?" he asked

95

himself, and thought that Salena was more intriguing than any mystery he could find in a book.

He knew he would never rest until he had discovered the whole story of her adventures.

There was no sign of her before dinner, and while the Duke changed into his evening-clothes, which he did whether he had company or was alone, he looked forward to talking to her.

It was therefore something of a disappointment when Dalton came into the Saloon to say:

"The young lady is asleep, Your Grace, and I thought it would be a mistake to awaken her."

"Of course it would, Dalton. The best thing that could happen is for her to sleep as long as possible."

"It's better than any tonic a Physician could prescribe, Your Grace."

"Then let her sleep, Dalton. She will feel all the better for it in the morning."

"I'm sure of that, Your Grace."

The Duke therefore had a lonely dinner, and when it was over he walked about on the deck until he too began to feel sleepy.

As he undressed and got into bed he told himself that he had enjoyed the day. It had in fact been quite different from any other day he had ever spent.

As Dalton was collecting his evening-clothes the Duke asked:

"There is no sound from Miss Salena? She has not woken?"

"I don't think she's moved, Your Grace. I peeped in a little while ago and she was sound asleep. I just slipped a hot-water bottle into her bed but didn't disturb her."

"Quite right, Dalton. I can always rely on you when anybody is unwell."

"It's easier to treat the body that the mind, Your Grace," Dalton replied.

This was indisputable, and the Duke got into bed determined to read. But he soon put aside his book and turned out the light to lie thinking about Salena.

He must have been asleep for an hour or more when something woke him.

He was suddenly alert but could hear nothing but the sound of the engines. Then it came again.

It was undoubtedly a scream.

The Duke switched on the light by his bed, and hearing Salena scream again and yet again, he jumped out of bed and ran to the next-door cabin.

As he opened the door he realised that Dalton had foolishly left her in darkness, but by the light streaming in from his own cabin he saw her run towards him.

She was wearing one of Imogen Moreton's night-gowns and as it was too long she tripped. As he put out his arms to steady her, she screamed:

"They are ... after ... me! They are ... going to ... catch me! Save ... me! Save ... me!"

She held on to him frantically, her fingers clutching at the folds of his nightshirt, and he held her against him.

"It is all right," he said gently, "you are dreaming. There is no-one to catch you. You are safe."

"They ... are ... there! I saw ... them!"

She gave another little scream that seemed to be strangled in her throat, and trembling violently she hid her face against the Duke's shoulder.

"You are quite safe here on the *Aphrodite*, Salena."

He felt that the name of the yacht penetrated her senses. Then suddenly like a child who has reached the end of her tether she burst into tears.

She cried tempestuously, the sobs wracking the whole of her body, her face still hidden in the Duke's shoulder.

Realising that she was past knowing where she was or what had happened to her, he picked her up in his arms.

For a moment he thought he would put her down on the bed, but she was holding on to him convulsively, as if he were a life-line from which she could not be separated.

Carrying her, he turned from her cabin and went into his own.

It was very large, stretching across the whole stern of the ship, with port-holes on either side of it. Against one wall was a comfortable sofa covered in velvet to match the head-board of the bed.

The Duke sat down, holding Salena in his arms and across his knees almost as if she were a baby.

She went on crying against his shoulder and he could feel her tears as they soaked through the thin silk of his nightshirt and onto his skin.

She was so slight and small that he felt she was in fact only a child who needed his protection, and his voice was very gentle as he said:

"There is no need to cry. Just trust me to help you and no-one will hurt you while you are here with me."

"They ... will ... guillotine m-me."

The words were whispered through her sobs and the Duke thought incredulously that he must have misunderstood what she had said.

"I ... k-killed him!" Salena went on, still in a low whisper. "I did not ... mean to ... but I picked up the ... paper-knife when I was trying to get away from him, and he ... he fell on ... it."

As if the picture of what had happened came back to her, she gave a stifled little scream.

"There was ... blood all over the ... bed ... and as he ... d-died, he said I had k-killed ... him."

The last words were almost incoherent, and now she was sobbing with an intensity that shook her whole body.

The Duke stroked her hair, which fell over her shoulders, and he realised that Imogen's nightgown, which was very daring and revealing, had left her arms bare and barely covered her breasts.

"Listen, Salena," he said. "I know whatever you did was an accident, and I promise that even if they

98

discover where you are, which is unlikely, you will
not be guillotined."

"B-but . . . I . . . I k-killed . . . him."

"If it was the man who beat you, then he deserved it."

It seemed as if the positive note in the Duke's
voice arrested her tears. Then she said:

"H-he . . . beat me . . . b-because I was . . . tr-try-
ing to run . . . away."

"Why?" the Duke asked.

He was almost afraid to ask questions or to do
anything but try to console her. This was the revela-
tion he had wanted to hear, and he was cautious lest
he might frighten her into silence again.

There was a moment's pause. Then Salena answered the question:

"H-he had a . . . wife and . . . ch-children."

"But you thought you loved him?" the Duke
asked.

She raised her face from his shoulder and looked
at him incredulously.

In the light from his bed-side lamp the Duke
could see the tears wet on her cheeks and standing
on the ends of her long eye-lashes.

Despite everything, she looked lovely, and yet
at the same time utterly pathetic, a lost waif, driv-
en by fear almost to the point of madness.

"He was . . . wicked . . . evil . . . old . . . and h-horri-
ble!" she said. "But he paid . . . P-Papa for me . . .
and there was . . . nothing . . . I could . . . do."

The tears flowed again but now she was crying
more quietly and the Duke felt that in a way they
were washing away some of the terror.

He was beginning to form a picture of what had
happened, and although there were still a hundred
questions he longed to ask, he knew that to do so
would be unwise.

He just held her close against him.

It flashed through his mind that this was the first
time in his life he had had a woman in his arms who

thought of him not as a man but just as an impersonal refuge against the terror that possessed her.

"You have been through so much," the Duke said quietly when he thought Salena's tears had abated. "What I suggest is that you go back to bed and try to sleep."

He felt her give a little shiver.

"I shall ... dream that ... they are trying to ... c-catch me.... I know they will be ... looking for me."

"You cannot be sure of that," the Duke replied. "And anyway, even if they are they will not find you. It was a million to one chance that I picked you up in the sea, and who could possibly suspect that that happened?"

"They ... will think I have ... drowned?" Salena asked, as if she formulated the idea to herself.

"I am sure of it," the Duke answered.

"And you will ... not let ... anyone know I am ... with you?"

"No-one shall know it."

She did not speak, and after a moment he said tentatively:

"When you feel like telling me the whole story, I shall be in the position to make discreet enquiries. After all, you are a very small person and it would be very difficult for you really to kill a man. He may not be dead."

"H-he ... said: 'You have ... killed me. I am ... dying!' He ... shut his ... eyes."

The words came jerkily from between Salena's lips.

"It must have been very frightening," the Duke said. "But trust me to find out the truth one day. I think you do trust me, Salena."

"It is ... wrong for ... you to be ... involved," she whispered.

"I will not be," the Duke replied, hoping his confidence was justified.

He realised that Salena was exhausted by her

tears, and now that she was no longer crying she seemed to be on the point of collapse.

"I am going to take you to bed," he said, "and I think perhaps it would be a good idea if I rang for Dalton to bring you some warm milk."

"No ... no!" Salena whispered, and he felt her pressing herself against him. "I do not ... want him to ... see me.... I just ... want to be with ... you."

He was well aware that she did not know what her words implied but was just clinging to him for safety.

With some agility he managed to rise to his feet without taking his arms from her.

"I am going to put you in your bed," he said, "and leave a light burning so that if you wake again it will not seem so dark or frightening. You know that I am only next door and will hear if you call me."

For a moment he thought she was going to say that she could not bear to be alone. Then she said in a child-like voice:

"Will you ... leave the door ... open?"

"I will leave your door open and mine," the Duke answered. "And let me tell you, I am a very light sleeper, so I shall hear you even if you whisper."

He carried her back into her cabin and set her down on the bed. He thought she trembled in the dark and hastily he reached out to switch on the light.

He saw her look round and said:

"You see, there is no-one here and actually nowhere anyone could hide. You are safe, Salena. Just keep saying to yourself: 'I am safe!' And remember, I am only next door."

She put her head on the pillow and he pulled the blankets over her.

She looked up at him and he had an almost irresistible impulse to bend down and kiss her. Then he knew it would not only frighten her but would destroy her confidence in him.

Instead, he smiled and said:

"Go to sleep, Salena. Remember, you have only to whisper and I will come to you."

"You are . . . quite . . . sure?"

She disengaged one of her hands from under the sheet which he had pulled right up to her chin and slipped it into his.

"You will . . . not go . . . away?" she asked a little incoherently.

"We are in the middle of the Mediterranean," he replied, "and it would be a very long swim before I could reach Spain!"

He smiled and added:

"Make no mistake about it, I shall be here in the morning."

He felt her fingers tighten for a moment on his; then, as if she was too exhausted even to continue to hold on to him, she relaxed and her eyes closed.

The Duke stood looking at her for a long moment. Then he turned very quietly and went from the cabin, leaving the door open.

As he got into bed he thought that never in his life had anything so strange happened to him.

He lay awake thinking over what Salena had revealed and trying to put all the pieces into place.

He thought now it incredible that she could have swum so far, for he was sure she had not been on a yacht and must therefore have come from one of the Villas which bordered on the sea outside Monte Carlo.

The *Aphrodite* had passed the great rock on which stood the Palace of Prince Charles, then there were the Villas below, and above was the road which went from Monte Carlo to Nice.

It was, the Duke reckoned, somewhere between Monte Carlo and Eze that they had found Salena, and he tried to remember the names of some of the people who owned Villas along that stretch of the coast.

He had been visiting Monte Carlo for some years,

but he had nearly always slept aboard his yacht in the harbour.

Although he had driven along the road, he was not as familiar with it as he might have been had he actually owned or stayed in one of the Villas.

The Marquess of Salisbury had built a huge Villa in the neighbourhood, but, the Duke remembered, it was not on sea-level.

It was impossible to imagine that Salena, wearing only a nightgown, could have climbed any distance down to the road, crossed it, then descended from there to the sea.

He was therefore certain that the Villa from which she had come must be on the sea side of both the road and the railway.

That, he thought, reduced his research considerably. At the same time, he was no wiser than he had been before.

"She is beginning to confide in me," he told himself. "Sooner or later she will tell me everything —even her name."

It seemed extraordinary that he should have held her so intimately in his arms, that he had actually seen her naked, that she had clung to him in desperation to save her from her dreams and her fears, but he still had no idea who she was.

There was no doubt that she was a lady, and he thought there was something very aristocratic in her small, perfect features, just as there was something exceedingly beautiful in every line of her body.

"She is unique," the Duke said to himself, "and if I were not a practical man I should be inclined to believe that she was in fact a reincarnation of Aphrodite, come back to earth with all the complications of love and treachery which are characteristic of Greek mythology."

He knew he ought to go to sleep, but as he turned over on his pillow he found that he was listening just in case Salena should call him.

He thought that no-one, least of all Imogen Moreton, would believe that a lovely woman had asked him to stay with her but he had carried her back to her bed and left her alone.

"She is far too innocent to realise what she asked," the Duke told himself.

At the same time, he remembered how he had wanted to kiss her.

He wondered if the man who had beaten her and betrayed her had kissed her passionately, and it made him feel angry to imagine such a thing.

If she had killed him it was exactly what he deserved.

"Blast the swine!" the Duke muttered. "If he is not dead already I would like the chance to kill him myself!"

Chapter Five

"Checkmate!"

It was a cry of triumph and Salena clapped her hands with delight as she exclaimed:

"I have won! I have won for the first time!"

The Duke looked at the chessboard with a puzzled expression on his face.

"I must have been asleep, or thinking about something else," he said, "to let you get past my guard."

"I really won?" Salena asked. "You were not being . . . generous?"

"Certainly not!" the Duke replied. "I like showing my superiority by invariably being the winner."

"But not this time!"

"No, you have won well and truly," he agreed.

She laughed again with sheer delight, and as she rose from the chess-table to walk to the window and look out into the garden he thought it was unbelievable what change there was in her appearance.

As if she was thinking almost the same thing, she said:

"It is so lovely here. Every time I look out at the flowers and the blue of the sea I think how lucky I am."

Then, before the Duke could speak, she said in a different tone:

"Do you realise we have been here nearly three weeks?"

The Duke found it hard to credit that so much time had passed since they had arrived in the harbour.

He and Salena had been on deck to watch the *Aphrodite* steam in amongst the Moroccan dhows sailing lazily up and down and trailing their nets as similar boats had done for two thousand years.

Salena's eyes had been on the great amphitheatre of hills glittering in the sunshine and the minarets rising high above the Sultan's Palace.

The Duke, however, pointed to where some distance from the town there were groves of orange trees and olive trees.

"My Villa is over there," he said, "and I think you will find it far more beautiful and certainly more comfortable than the Sultan's Palace."

In consequence, Salena had expected something exceptional, perhaps on the same pattern as the Prince's Villa in Monte Carlo.

In fact she found what appeared to be a Palace in itself. Built in the Moorish style, with court-yards, cool verandahs, and innumerable rooms, it occupied a great acreage of ground.

It was surrounded by a garden that was so breathtakingly lovely that she had no words in which to extol it.

The Duke explained that his father had spent the last years of his life in Tangier and had bought the Villa standing on the present site to extend and enlarge it.

The garden was already exceptional, but he had devoted a great deal of time to it and had made it one of the most beautiful places in the whole of Morocco.

In fact, the Duke had not visited the Villa for two years, but he had no need to worry as to whether it was well looked after.

Soon after he inherited the title, the Curator at

Combe, who was getting on in years, was told by his Doctor that if he wished to live he must move to a warmer climate.

Therefore, the Duke had sent Mr. Warren and his wife out to Tangier, with nothing more arduous to do than to keep the Villa ready in case at any time he wished to go there.

If he had not had Salena with him, he would in his usual fashion have taken the Warrens by surprise.

But because he wished there to be no difficulties or discomforts where she was concerned, he had cabled them when the ship reached Gibraltar.

One glance at the Villa was enough to tell him that it had been unnecessary to announce his arrival.

The walls had been newly painted, the rooms were aired and well looked after, and the garden was even more exotic than he remembered it.

He thought that after even a few days the beauty of Salena's surroundings was sweeping away her fears and she was beginning to change back to what he guessed she must have been like before her terrible experience in Monte Carlo.

After she had told him so much that night when she had cried in his arms, it was easy for him to extract from her the rest of the story almost without her being aware of it.

What she did not tell him was very obvious to the Duke.

He could understand that, having no experience of men or indeed of the Social World at Monte Carlo, she had found it at first bewildering and then terrifying.

She was affected all the more since she had previously been so cloistered and sheltered.

Yet, any girl of eighteen, even if more sophisticated, would have been disgusted and mentally upset by the treatment which had been meted out to Salena.

And the Duke realised that Salena's extraordi-

nary endurance in swimming as far as she had was
the direct result of being activated by a violent and
unnatural emotion.

It was much the same, he told himself, as what
happened to a man who was angry: simply because
he was so emotionally aroused, he was able to fight
with a greater strength than had been deemed possible.

After such an experience, a certain degree of
mental and physical collapse was inevitable.

The Duke was wise enough to realise that it
would be a long time before Salena was completely
healed and the horrors that had been inflicted upon
her were forgotten.

Nothing could be more conducive to this than
to be at the Villa with no-one but himself and his
soft-footed Moroccan servants, who, under the tutor-
age of Mr. Warren, were able to make themselves almost invisible.

It was like being alone on an enchanted island,
the Duke thought, but what was romantic in theory
could often prove in practice extremely boring.

However, he found not only that boredom was
impossible for him when he was with Salena, but
that every day he grew more interested in her and
entranced by her.

Eventually she had described more or less everything that had happened after her arrival in Monte
Carlo, with the warnings of the nuns ringing in her
ears.

She told him how she had expected to find the
station itself looking strange and sinister.

Two of the things, however, she still kept secret
—her own identity and that of the man who had deceived her into a false marriage.

It puzzled the Duke that she would not trust him
completely, but he did not understand that Salena
was in fact protecting her father.

The morning after she had been rescued by the
Duke, she had taken herself to task for having said

so much and revealing a great deal that she had intended to keep hidden forever.

She was certain that it would be disloyal and extremely wrong if she revealed to the Duke that her father had been involved in doing anything so shameful as to sell her to the Prince.

They were acquaintances, if not friends, and she knew that the Duke could in fact do her father inestimable harm socially if he wished to.

"He must never know who I am," Salena told herself.

Moreover, to let the Duke know that it was the Prince who had treated her so brutally might also involve her father.

'Mama told me to look after Papa,' she thought, 'and so Papa must never learn that I am ... alive, and never, never ... be aware that it was the Duke who befriended me.'

She did not ask herself how she would disappear when the Duke was no longer willing to protect her.

He was beginning to assume a position of more and more importance in her life, so that it was hard for her even to visualise existing if he was not there.

Besides her fear of the Prince and of all men like him, there was also an anxiety about her future, which she tried to hide away at the back of her mind.

She told herself that it should not spoil her present happiness or the joy of being in such a wonderful place.

Every night when she said her prayers she thanked God for saving her and for letting it be the Duke and the *Aphrodite*, who had come to her rescue.

Yet, the thought of other men could still be terrifying, and because of it she had no wish to wander through the Medina, where she knew there were booths that sold the fascinating Moroccan crafts which she had read about in books.

She wanted to see things but not people, and something very sensitive within her shrank for the moment from contact with everyone except the Duke.

He understood what she was feeling and was in fact extremely relieved that he did not have to trail her, as other women might have expected, through the narrow, airless streets.

He disliked being pestered to buy cheap jewellery, pottery, spices, and carpets, for which he had no use.

The last time he had come to the Villa he had brought with him a beautiful Socialite who had been one of Imogen's predecessors.

She had wanted everything she saw, and while it amused him to pander to her greed, he had no desire to repeat the performance.

Instead, he took Salena driving away from the city, to the fertile plains occupied by the Moorish tribes.

She was thrilled with her first sight of pomegranate trees, with the date-palms, walnuts, figs, and olives, and with the colourful appearance of the people they passed on the road.

The Duke had pointed out to her the water-sellers, clad in bright red and carrying on their backs a goatskin on which the hair still hung, swollen with water.

The women, veiled and anonymous in their *djellabas,* and the men, in their red fez hats, baggy green pantaloons, and yellow slippers, made her feel as if they were all part of a fairy-story.

The Duke, who was extremely well informed, told her about the Berbers, a magnificent, age-old, mysterious race which had lived in North Africa, especially amongst the mountains, since the dawn of time.

Salena listened attentively as he explained that a Berber was tall, courageous, often a brilliant linguist and a great agriculturalist.

"It should interest you to know," he ended with a smile, "that St. Augustine, amongst other notable men, was a Berber."

It was something very new to the Duke to find that a woman wished to talk to him intellectually, and most unusual of all was that she wanted him to impart knowledge which did not concern her personally.

He found it a revealing experience and an extremely fascinating one to talk while Salena listened to him, her eyes on his face, her mind absorbing everything he said.

Sometimes he tested her a day or so later to see if she had really listened to and understood what he had told her.

He invariably found that not only did she remember what he had said, but she had thought about it and added her own ideas, so that they could discuss together what she had learnt.

'We have been here three weeks,' the Duke repeated to himself.

He was sitting back in his chair and looking at Salena silhouetted against the sunshine.

If anyone had told him a few months ago that he would be alone with a woman for three weeks and the time passed so quickly that it might have been three days, he would not have believed it.

Even in his most ardent affairs, when he was not actually making love with the object of his affections, he found that time seemed heavy on his hands and he wanted to employ himself in other ways.

But here, surprisingly, every moment seemed a delight and indeed different from the moment before.

He had been with Salena all the time, and had not left her even to go riding as he would have done had anyone else been with him.

He told himself that it was because he knew she would be afraid in his absence.

From the moment he had begun to see the difference in her, he was determined she should not relapse into the state she had been in when he had first found her.

But he was now honest enough to admit that it was more than that.

He was concerned not only with Salena's health and her mental attitude towards life but with his own feelings about her.

He shied away from admitting that he was in love.

But ever since the night when he had wanted to kiss her because she had been so pathetic, the desire not only to kiss her but to hold her in his arms and to make love to her had been a constant and ever-increasing temptation.

Having been very spoilt where women were concerned, and having always been the hunted rather than the hunter, the Duke had never had to control his desires or deny his passions.

But with Salena he knew that one unwary word, one action that was not restrained, would shatter her faith and confidence in him and bring back the terror which was not far beneath the surface.

He therefore forced an iron control upon himself and a discipline that was something so new and so unusual that sometimes he laughed mockingly at his own efforts.

And yet he knew that to hurt Salena after she had been frightened so terribly by her father, and by the unknown man who had pretended to marry her, would be an act of betrayal for which he would never be able to forgive himself.

'I love her!' he thought now. 'I love her in a way that I have never loved a woman before.'

He was in fact surprised at his own capability of feeling so intensely and so deeply.

It was almost as if he said, as other lovers had said since the beginning of time: "This is different. I had not realised love could be like this."

But it was in fact the truth. It *was* different!

Never before had the Duke wanted to protect a woman, to look after her; never had he been concerned not with his own feelings but with hers.

Never had love seemed more spiritual than physical, and yet he knew that his need for Salena was like a fire burning inside himself, always growing in intensity.

She turned from the garden to come back towards the Duke.

The huge room in which they were sitting was very cool, and it was decorated with the most exquisite mosaics.

There were rugs which were so precious that they should have been hung like tapestries on the walls, and comfortable low sofas piled with colorful cushions.

It was a room made for relaxation besides containing some unique treasures, which Salena had handled with awe and admiration.

"When it grows cooler," she said to the Duke, "could we climb down to the beach? It is so lovely by the sea."

There was a twisting, rather dangerous path by which they could descend the cliffs, and the Duke would take his exercise by climbing down it with Salena, then walking for miles along the golden sands when the sun had lost its heat.

"I believe that the only reason why you want to look at the sea is that you are longing to swim in it," he replied.

"It would be lovely to swim with you," she answered.

"I have been thinking that I might build a swimming-bath," the Duke said, "and in fact I have already discussed it with Mr. Warren."

"A swimming-bath!" Salena exclaimed. "That would be wonderful! I have not swum in one since I was at Bath. There the water is naturally warm."

"The water is warm here from the heat of the sun," the Duke said. "In fact, the difficulty will be to keep it cool."

"When could the bath be ready?" Salena asked.

He laughed.

"It will take time. Nothing is done quickly in Arab countries."

He saw the excitement fade from her face and knew that she was thinking she would not be there to see it completed.

He did not speak, and after a moment Salena said:

"I was ... thinking last night that ... soon you will want ... to leave."

"Why should you think that?" the Duke enquired.

"Dalton was saying that he had never known you to stay here, or at any other place, for so long. He was not ... complaining; he ... just likes being here."

"I am glad it pleases him," the Duke replied. "But what about you?"

"You know I love it. It is the most wonderful place I could imagine! It is like stepping into Paradise."

She glanced out the window, then back at him.

"But I would be ... happy anywhere in the world ... if I was with ... you."

She spoke quite spontaneously, as a child might have done, and the Duke realised once again how difficult it was to gauge exactly what she felt about him as a man.

He supposed that because she had been in a Convent for the last two years and had had no experience of men, she had no sense of coquetry.

It never seemed to strike her that she should try to attract him as a man.

There was, too, the natural reaction from being assaulted by a brute whose only thought of her had been one of lust, so that she shrank from anything which might involve her considering herself as a woman.

"Does she love me?" the Duke asked himself, as he had asked himself a thousand times every day and every night.

There was no mistaking the joy that Salena showed in his company.

He had learnt from the very first that it was impossible for her to hide her feelings, and when he came into the room her face lit up as though there were a thousand candles inside her.

Then she would run towards him spontaneously and slip her hand into his.

She talked with him easily, unaffectedly, and without any sign of self-consciousness.

He came into her bed-room to say good-night to her, and it never occurred to her that it was in any way reprehensible or even unconventional.

The Duke was quite convinced that it was because she had turned to him for protection and he was now a symbol of the only thing which was stable in her life.

But it never crossed her mind for one moment that he might be a potential lover.

She came nearer to him and, as she so often did, sat down on the ground at his feet.

"There are so many things I would like to do with you," she said, as if she was thinking aloud. "You said I was to wait until I was well enough, and I am well now, really well, I promise you."

"Then what would you like to do?" the Duke asked.

As she raised her flower-like face to his, he thought she grew more lovely every day.

There was an ethereal look about her, and she had no awareness of how alluring and enticing she was.

In a way, the Duke thought, he could understand the man who had bought her from her father, desiring her to the point where he lost all control of himself.

Because she was near to him now, he could feel his heart thumping against his breast and a throbbing at his temples.

It was with the greatest difficulty that he prevented himself from putting out his arms and lifting her close against him, as he had done when she cried despairingly against his shoulder.

He was afraid that if he did so now he would see the happy expression in her eyes turn to one of horror and she would run away from him like a hunted animal, perhaps to fling herself into the sea as she had done before.

"What do you want to do?" he asked again, controlling his voice.

She held up her ringless left hand to count on her fingers:

"One ... I would like to swim with you," she said. "Two ... I would like to ride, as you promised we would. Three ... I want to explore with you the mountains that lie beyond the plain and where you tell me I shall see a part of the real Morocco where the tourists never penetrate."

"That is quite a programme," the Duke said in an amused voice. "Anything else?"

Salena threw wide her arms.

"Dozens and dozens of things," she replied. "I will write them all down if you like. There are things I want you to tell me, to teach me; and the world is very big."

"By that remark I imagine you are insinuating that the *Aphrodite* is in the harbour waiting to carry us to other lands."

Salena drew in her breath.

"I know that is only an ... impossible ... dream," she said, "but sometimes before I go to sleep I pretend that we are ... steaming away into the unknown to find an ... ancient land that has never been ... discovered before."

"There are not many of them," the Duke replied, "and perhaps we are already in a land which is less developed than any other."

"Why is that?" Salena enquired.

"One reason is that the desert plateaux are occupied by fierce tribes of bandits, and murders are rife," the Duke replied.

"Then we will not go there," Salena said quickly. "Supposing you were held captive or ... murdered ... I could not bear it!"

There was a throb in her voice which the Duke found very moving.

"I wonder if you would really mind ..." he began to say.

Then before he could complete the sentence the curtain which covered one of the entrances to the room was swept aside and a native servant bowed someone in.

For a moment the Duke stared incredulously at the newcomer.

Too late he realised that he should have given instructions that he was not at home to visitors and had no intention of receiving any.

He had never imagined that any of his friends would know where he was, and now it was too late.

It was Imogen who was moving towards him— Imogen, with a smile on her beautiful face.

She was looking extremely elegant and sophisticated in a gown that cried "Paris" and a hat that must have astounded the Moroccans as they saw her driving to the Villa.

"Are you surprised to see me, Hugo?" she asked.

There was a note in her voice which told him she did not expect him to be surprised so much as delighted.

Slowly the Duke rose to his feet and as he did so Salena sprang to hers.

For a moment she looked at the elegant woman advancing towards them, then swiftly and silently she turned and ran out through another entrance.

Imogen Moreton looked after her, a question in her eyes.

"Who was that?" she enquired.

There was a sharp note in her voice which the Duke did not miss.

"Why are you here?" he parried.

"I guessed this was where you would come," Imogen answered.

She reached the Duke and threw back her head in her characteristic manner to look up at him.

"How could you have been so cruel, so unkind, as to leave me in such a way?" she asked softly. "It was so unlike you, Hugo, that I knew I had to come here to tell you so."

"Who brought you?" the Duke asked.

Imogen gave a low laugh.

"There is no need to be jealous, dearest. It was not the Grand Duke."

She gave him a glance from under her long eyelashes and added:

"They told me at Boris's Villa that you had gone into the garden to look for me but had not returned, so I guessed what had happened."

She made an expressive gesture with her hands.

"Surely, knowing all we have meant to each other for so long, you could not really be angry at something so trivial, so completely unimportant, as a kiss?"

The Duke did not answer.

He was in fact wondering how he had ever thought Imogen so attractive.

There was, he decided, something so artificial and insincere about her that it was astounding that he had not noticed it before.

He said:

"I am sorry you have come all this way to explain something which really does not need any explanation."

"What do you mean by that?"

"I mean," the Duke said slowly, "that we are

both sophisticated people. I am very grateful, Imogen, for the happiness you gave me and for the delightful times we had together, but they are over."

He saw by the astonishment on her face that she had not imagined for a moment that their liaison was really at an end.

For one thing, she was too conceited to think that any man would tire of her before she tired of him.

The Duke was certain that she had convinced herself that he had gone away in a fit of jealousy and she had only to appear to make him realise that life was intolerable without her.

"You cannot mean that, Hugo!" she said in a shocked tone.

"We had much better be frank about these things," the Duke replied.

With an effort Imogen forced a coaxing note in her voice as she said:

"You are still angry with me, and that is very foolish of you because you know I love you and there is no other man in my life."

She saw that he was unconvinced and added quickly:

"No-one could take the Grand Duke seriously, and you cannot allow him to spoil the happiness that we have found this last year."

The Duke did not reply and after a moment she said:

"If I had a tiny flirtation with Boris it was only because you did not appear to want me with you for —ever. You did not ask me, dearest Hugo, to be your wife."

She moved a little closer to him, expecting him to put his arms round her, and her lips were ready for his.

The Duke turned away abruptly to go to a desk which stood by one wall of the room.

"I will give you a cheque, Imogen," he said, "to compensate you for any inconvenience I may have caused by my precipitate departure. You will also find your clothes and jewels waiting for you on the *Aphrodite*. You doubtless saw her when you came into the harbour."

"I not only saw your yacht, but I have already been aboard her," Imogen replied. "I could not believe that you meant to deprive me of the jewels you have given me, which I value because they expressed your love."

The Duke had sat down and opened a chequebook.

As if she suddenly realised that the softness of her voice and the blandishments she was using were having no effect, she stamped her foot.

"I do not want your money, Hugo, I want you! Stop pretending! You can send for my luggage, and we will be happy together as we have always been."

"I am not pretending," the Duke said harshly. "Nor am I inviting you to stay here as my guest."

"Hugo!" The word seemed to ring round the room.

"I am sorry if I am upsetting you," the Duke said, still with his back to her, "but I meant it when I said that anything we felt for each other in the past is now over and finished."

"I do not believe you!" Imogen cried. "You are merely behaving like this because you want me to go down on my knees and apologise for letting Boris kiss me. It meant nothing! Boris is Boris, and you were amusing yourself at the gambling-tables. Why should I not have a little fun?"

"I am not reproaching you," the Duke said wearily.

He rose from the desk, holding the cheque in his hand, and came towards her.

"Take this, Imogen," he said, "and let me once again thank you for the past, and do your best to forget me in the future."

"Forget you?" she screamed.

At the same time, her hand went out and took the cheque from the Duke.

She looked at it and he knew that she had intended to tear it up until she saw the very considerable sum inscribed on it.

"Do you really think you can live without me?" she asked in a different tone.

"I am as sure of that as I am sure that you can live without me," the Duke replied.

Imogen raised her eyes from the cheque to say:

"I always thought, Hugo, that eventually we would marry each other. We are so suited in every way."

"I would not be the right husband for you," the Duke said firmly.

Imogen sighed.

"I suppose you are not the marrying sort, although there will always be women in your life. What does that girl—for she looked little more than a child—mean to you?"

"She is my concern, not yours."

"I have seen her somewhere before," Imogen said, wrinkling her white brow with an effort at trying to remember.

"You have?" the Duke questioned.

He wanted to ask Imogen where she had seen Salena and if she knew her name.

Then he told himself he would not spy on someone he loved, and certainly would not involve Imogen of all people in Salena's secret.

"I am sure you have a carriage waiting for you," he said. "Or would you wish me to provide one?"

"Are you really sending me away, Hugo? I just cannot believe it!"

Her tone sounded incredulous. At the same time, the Duke noticed cynically that she slipped his cheque into the little silk purse which hung by ribbons from her wrist.

"I think it would be uncomfortable for both of

us to rake over the past and perhaps spoil the things we wish to remember," the Duke said. "I am sure in the years to come everything will sink into its right perspective and we can be friends."

"I have no wish to be friends with you, Hugo," Imogen retorted. "I love you, and you said over and over again how much you love me."

The Duke did not answer, and as if she realised it was hopeless she said:

"Very well, but I cannot help feeling that you will be sorry, that you have dispensed with me quite unnecessarily. You were jealous—absurdly and quite ridiculously jealous!"

She paused, and when he did not contradict her she went on:

"Because you will not admit that it was wrong and extremely unchivalrous of you to leave Monte Carlo as you did, you are now cutting me out of your life."

It was an explanation, the Duke thought, which she would give herself to put him in the wrong and to avoid taking any of the blame for what had occurred.

"It may seem ridiculous to you, Imogen," he said, "but it is a fact, and you were always very courageous in facing the truth in the past."

This was not so, but he told himself that it would be a sop to her pride that he thought so.

"If you do not want me, Hugo," Imogen said, tossing her head, "there are plenty of other men who do."

She half-turned away from him, then said:

"Shall we kiss each other good-bye, for old times' sake?"

It was a last effort, the Duke knew, to arouse him as she had always been able to do before, and to recapture him despite himself.

"I think it would be far more natural," he said with a note of amusement in his voice, "for me to

escort you to your carriage and for us to part in a
friendly fashion."

"Very well, if that is what you want."

Affronted and piqued, Imogen flounced across
the room, waiting only for the Duke to draw the
curtain aside.

She did not speak again until after they had
traversed the long corridors and reached the front
door.

There were a number of servants in attendance,
but before she stepped into her carriage, which had
a white linen awning to protect her from the sun, she
held out one gloved hand with an imperious gesture.

"Good-bye, Hugo," she said. "If you regret your
decision before I leave the harbour, it need only be
au revoir."

The Duke took her hand and raised it perfunc-
torily to his lips, but he did not reply.

He was aware that she was really pleading with
him for another chance, but he knew as she drove
away that he had no wish ever to see her again.

It was Salena who had shown him how false and
superficial Imogen was and that the feelings he had
had for her were not worthy to be called love.

As he walked slowly back to the Sitting-Room he
thought that if he had changed Salena's life, she had
certainly changed him.

He saw now how he had accepted false values,
the spurious and second-rate, and what was so reprehensible was that he had not realised he was doing so.

It was Salena's purity, innocence, and deeply ingrained faith in God which had pointed the way to
a very different sense of values which the Duke had
in fact not contemplated since he was very young.

Once, he supposed, he had been extremely ideal-
istic and thought of himself as the champion of everything that was fine and noble.

He remembered when he was at Oxford thinking that when he inherited he would use his position to alter so many things in Imperialist Britain that needed reforming.

He had had a small circle of friends and they had sat up at night, after their studies were over, replanning the world.

They discussed the injustices of the law, and the neglect, privation, and starvation which still existed in Britain despite the fact that it was the richest country in Europe.

They had been, the Duke thought, like Crusaders, dedicating themselves to a Holy War against not the Infidel but everything that demanded the challenge of fresh minds.

They were prepared to fight for what was right and ready to challenge what was wrong.

Looking back, he could see how easily he had been diverted from the course he had set himself.

He had come into the Dukedom, and there were so many people willing to show him how to be amused and entertained and to help him spend his huge fortune.

There were his race-horses, vast covert shoots at which the Prince was eager to be a guest, entertainments which seemed almost compulsory in London, and in the country innumerable problems that appertained to his estates.

Gradually he lost touch with his Oxford friends, or else like him they had taken the easy course of swimming with the social tide and not against it.

It was Salena, the Duke thought now, who had shown him the way back.

He wondered what she would think of Imogen and was afraid that her unexpected appearance might have upset her.

She was not in the Sitting-Room, and he went in search of her, being sure she would be in her bedroom. It was a large room, next to his own because Salena was still afraid of her dreams.

She was sitting in the window and as the Duke

entered she turned her face to him and he saw that he was right in thinking that Imogen had upset her.

"She has gone," he announced, as if Salena had asked him the question, "and she will not come back."

He joined Salena on the window-seat as he spoke and sat down on the soft cushions which covered it.

Then as he looked at her expression he asked:

"What is worrying you?"

"I ... did not ... think there were ... women in your life like ... that."

It was an answer he had not expected, and because he had to think how to reply to it, he said evasively:

"I am not certain I understand what you are implying."

"When I first ... saw you in the ... Casino ..."

"You saw me in the Casino?" the Duke interrupted. "You never told me that."

"I saw you walking through the crowd alone," Salena said quickly, "but I supposed there would be lovely women covered in jewels ... waiting for you."

"Why did you think that?"

"I do not ... know. I just thought it. Then when you were alone on the yacht and were so kind to me ... I imagined you were different from the ... the men I have met, who only ... laugh, drink, and ... gossip about each other."

"I am different!" the Duke said firmly. "And Lady Moreton, for that is who has just called here, means nothing now in my life."

"She is ... very beautiful," Salena said.

The Duke realised she was comparing herself with Imogen and that it was the first time she had ever been self-conscious, that she had ever thought of herself as competing in his eyes with another member of her sex.

Then he thought that Imogen had brought a harsh wind of reality into their enchanted island, and he cursed himself for not having taken precautions against unwanted visitors.

125

Because he loved Salena and because he was afraid of the expression in her eyes he said:

"I am a man, Salena, and I think it would insult your intelligence if I told you there had not been women in my life since I grew up."

There was silence and the Duke hardly dared to look to see how Salena had taken this. Then she said in a lost little voice:

"I ... I suppose I should have ... known that! I know it is what other ... men are like ... even ..."

She stopped.

She had been about to say "even Papa," but instead, after a perceptible pause, she went on:

"It is just that you ... seemed so different. I had not ... thought of you in ... that way. It was very ... stupid of me."

"Not stupid," the Duke said. "I think in these past few weeks, Salena, we have both discovered new things about each other and about ourselves."

He chose his words with care as he went on:

"If I never saw you again after today, I know that what you have meant to me would still remain and alter my life as I intend it to do."

He smiled, as he went on:

"I feel in some way as if until you were with me I was just floundering about, trying to make up my mind what course I should take, and finding it difficult to decide which would be the best one."

"You mean ... a way of ... living?" Salena asked.

"Exactly!" the Duke agreed. "Now, after all our discussions—and we have talked of many serious things together, Salena—I intend to live in a very different manner from the way I have before."

As he spoke he was surprised at his own decision.

He had known that he wanted things to be different, as he wanted Salena herself, but he had not actually formulated his decision in words.

"There are a great many things to do in England," he said, "which I should have attended to a long time ago. When I return I shall look into them very closely and spend a great deal more time than I have done hitherto in the political world."

"I am sure that is . . . right for you," Salena said. "You are not only so . . . important . . . you are so . . . clever . . . and you have such a . . . brilliant mind."

The Duke smiled.

"I hope you are right. Not everybody shares your belief in me."

"They will," Salena said. "I am sure of that."

He wanted to tell her there and then that he needed her help and inspiration, but he felt as if the shadow of Imogen still stood between them. After a moment he said:

"I think it would be a good idea if tonight we discussed the things that we feel should be done, and perhaps we can make a list of them."

"You mean things like the . . . reformation of the Children's Employment Act?" Salena asked.

"Exactly!" the Duke replied.

"I learnt at the Convent how terribly badly paid the seamstresses are in France," Salena said reflectively. "The Mother Superior who used to lecture to us on these things said that in England there are women who sew buttons on shirts and have to complete thousands a week even to make a few pence to save themselves from starvation."

"Those are the sort of things we must look into and see what can be done about them," the Duke said with a note of determination in his voice.

He looked out the window.

"It is growing cooler," he said. "Shall we go into the garden?"

He rose to his feet and put his hand out towards Salena.

He thought that she hesitated for a second before taking it eagerly, as she would have done an hour or so ago.

Because he loved her, because he was unusually perceptive where she was concerned, he knew that

127

since Imogen had intruded on them things had changed.

Salena was for the first time thinking of him as having the passions and desires of a man.

Chapter Six

Salena walked across the Sitting-Room, touching first one thing, then another.

The Duke watched her with a speculative look in his eyes.

He knew that two days ago she would have been sitting at his feet, talking to him eagerly and unaffectedly, like a child.

But since Imogen had come to the Villa he had known there was a constriction in her attitude which had not been there before.

She still listened to him intently and he still saw her eyes light up whenever he came into the room; at the same time, he was aware that she was more tense than she had been before Imogen's intrusion.

"You are very restless," he said now. "Perhaps it is time we left Tangier for 'pastures new.'"

He had meant his words to startle her and he certainly succeeded.

She turned round, her eyes wide and questioning, then moved swiftly across the room to stand beside him.

"Do you . . . want to go . . . away?" she asked.

"I was thinking of you," he said. "Somehow you seem bored, which you have never seemed to be before."

"Of course I am not bored!" she said passionately. "How could I be bored when I am with you? It is just ..."

Her voice died away and after a moment the Duke asked:

"It is just—what?"

Salena sat down on the floor beside him. She did not look at him but was staring ahead, as if she was choosing her words with care.

"It is just," she said in a low voice, "that I cannot help ... feeling you might want to be with your ... friends and are only staying ... here to be ... kind to me."

"In the past," the Duke replied, "I have often been accused of being selfish, and thinking about my own interests rather than those of other people."

He smiled as he went on:

"Will it reassure you to know that I am very happy here and that when I am prepared to move I shall say so without any reservation, or should I say without consideration for you or anyone else."

Salena raised her head to look at him.

"Is that ... really true?" she questioned.

"I assure you that when possible I always speak the truth," the Duke replied loftily. "Lying involves one in so much unnecessary trouble."

"I am sure that is true," Salena agreed, "and I am happy, so very happy, to be here. But the ... time must come when you will ... have to go ... back."

He knew she was wondering what would become of her when that happened, and he replied:

"Let us leave that moment until it confronts us. I cannot imagine a more beautiful or more desirable place than Morocco to be in at this time of the year."

He saw that he had reassured her, at any rate for the moment.

As she smiled at him he saw that the shadow had gone from her eyes and there was almost a radiance about her.

"Then if we are staying," Salena said, "may I please ride with you this afternoon or tomorrow morning?"

The Duke was just about to reply when a servant came into the room.

"What is it?" the Duke asked impatiently as the man bowed politely.

"There is a lady to see you, Master. She says it is of the utmost importance."

"A lady?" the Duke queried.

"The lady who called the day before yesterday. She seems very agitated."

The Duke frowned.

He had given instructions that whoever called he was not to be disturbed, and never again under any pretext was a visitor to be shown unannounced into the Sitting-Room.

He was well aware, however, that if Imogen wished to see him she would be so insistent that the servants would be overpowered by her.

He was certain too that if Imogen was intent on talking to him she would not leave until she had done so.

Before he rose to his feet he put out his hand and laid it on Salena's shoulder.

"This will not take long," he said. "And I will order the horses so that we can ride today as soon as the sun has lost its strength."

"That will be wonderful!" she cried.

But he knew that as she watched him cross the room the shadows were back in her eyes.

As soon as she was alone Salena rose to her feet.

She felt perturbed and there was a pain in her breast that had not been there before.

Why had the beautiful Lady Moreton, who had called to see the Duke the day before yesterday, come again? What did she want with him? And why, if she was so intent on seeing him, had she not asked him to call on her?

These were questions she could not answer, and

she moved through the open window onto the verandah outside.

The garden was very lovely in the sunlight,
but for the first time it failed to evoke a response in
Salena.

She could think only of a beautiful face turned
appealingly towards the Duke, and knew that in contrast to the sophistication and *chic* of his visitor she
felt drab and inconspicuous.

Because it was impossible to sit still, she walked
to the far end of the verandah to look out not at the
sea but at the mountains rising blue and purple
against the sky.

They were wonderfully impressive, but again it
did nothing to erase the pain Salena was feeling or
the agitation within her that seemed to increase every moment.

Suddenly she heard a sound in the garden. It
was not loud, but it seemed like the cry of a small
animal in pain.

She listened, wondering vaguely what it could be.
Then it came again and again.

She located it in some flowering shrubs which
grew in exotic profusion only a few yards from the
verandah.

'There must be an animal caught in a trap,' she
thought.

She looked about for a gardener to whom she
could call for assistance, but, seeing no sign of anyone, she ran down the steps of the verandah and
across the lawn towards the shrubs.

The animal was still crying. Then as she parted
the branches with their heavy-scented blossoms she
herself gave a shrill scream.

A black cloth was thrown over her head, covering
her completely, and she was picked up in strong
arms and carried away.

After the first scream Salena was stunned into silence, besides being stifled by the heaviness of the
cloth which covered her.

She tried to struggle but it seemed as if she were encompassed about by innumerable iron bands. Only after a few seconds did she realise that they were the arms of the men who carried her.

With an effort, feeling as if it was almost impossible to breathe, she tried again to scream, but it was impossible.

She found too that she could not move her arms, and her ankles were held by strong fingers that bit into her flesh.

She was carried some distance while she tried frantically to guess what had happened and also to keep breathing.

She felt as if she must faint or become unconscious not only because it was so difficult to breathe but because the grip of the arms holding her was extremely painful.

Then suddenly there was a chatter of voices in Arabic and she was put down on the ground; but before she could make an effort to move, a rope was wound round her, keeping her hands to her sides, while another rope tied her legs together.

She was picked up once again, and now surprisingly she found herself seated in what seemed to be a chair.

She was being lashed to it with more ropes; someone was giving orders; and as she rocked backwards and forwards she realised incredibly that she was on the back of a camel.

There was no mistaking the uncomfortable angle at which the howdah in which she was sitting moved as the camel rose to its feet.

A howdah was, she knew, a kind of sedan chair made of coloured wicker with a curtained awning above her head.

The camel walked forward at first slowly, then quicker, and she guessed from the sound that there were other camels moving beside her.

She could hardly believe that only a moment ago she had been in the safety and security of the

Villa, with the Duke beside her, and because she was
with him she was happy.

Now she was being carried away, and she thought
despairingly that he would never know where she
had gone.

It made her feel panic-stricken and she tried
again to scream, but the sound was lost in the folds
of the black cloth through which she could not see
and in the sounds of the camels' hoofs on stones and
gravel.

'They are taking me away! Save me! Save me!'
Salena cried out in her heart, but she knew there was
no possibility of the Duke hearing such an ineffectual cry for help.

Then it struck her that she was being abducted
for ransom.

She remembered that one evening when they
were having dinner the Duke had been talking of
Europeans who had attractive houses on the higher
altitudes in the vicinity of Tangier.

"One of them, a rich man," he had said, "was
kidnapped a year or so ago by Moorish Berbers."

"How frightening!" Salena had exclaimed. "Did
he escape?"

"He was released when the brigands obtained
some concessions from the Moorish Government."

"They did not hurt him?"

"No, apparently they treated him quite well,
but because they got what they wanted it has
made other residents nervous and feel obliged to
worry over their own security."

"You are ... safe?" Salena had asked breathlessly.

The Duke smiled to himself because her thoughts
were for him and not, as any other guest might have
reacted, for herself.

"I assure you," he replied, "that Mr. Warren has
not only chosen the servants who work here with
great care, but when my yacht is in the harbour several of my crew are also in attendance on me."

Salena knew that this was true.

The Duke's valet looked after him, and the delicious food they ate was a predominately French cuisine, due to the capable hands of the Chef on the yacht.

As he picked up his glass of wine the Duke thought there was still a slight look of worry in Salena's expressive eyes.

"You are not to perturb yourself about me or be afraid," he commanded. "I would not have told you the story had I thought it would make you anxious."

"I am not anxious about myself," Salena answered. "No-one would wish to kidnap me and expect a ransom. But . . . you are different."

Now, incredibly, it was she who had been kidnapped, not the Duke, and she thought how much she would resent his having to pay a large sum for her release.

'Why . . . oh why . . . do such terrible things . . . happen to me?' she asked herself.

She wondered how long it would be before the Duke found that she was missing. Then her captors would demand ransom money.

He would be angry, she knew, not because of the price asked, whatever it might be, but because it would infuriate him to give in to brigands and robbers and provide them with an incentive to abduct other victims.

Suddenly she asked herself in a panic if perhaps he would decide to teach the brigands a lesson by refusing to accede to their demands.

Horrified by this idea, she struggled violently again the ropes that bound her arms to the sides of her body and to the howdah.

She was far too weak and the ropes were too thick and strong for the effort to make her feel anything but more helpless and more breathless than she had before.

The camel which carried her was not moving as quickly as it had a few minutes before and she knew it was because they were climbing uphill.

They must be leaving the valley of the city, and Salena felt that if once they got amongst the thick trees which covered the lower part of the mountains, it would be impossible for the Duke ever to find her again, even if he wished to.

There was nothing she could do but pray, and her prayers seemed muddled into an appeal both to God and to the Duke himself.

'Save ... me! Save ... me!'

She repeated and re-repeated the words over and over again in her mind, her whole being yearning towards him.

She thought that somehow, by some supernatural method, she must reach him simply because she needed him so desperately.

'I want you ... I want ... you. ...'

She repeated the words to herself and remembered how he had held her in his arms as she cried against his shoulder on the yacht.

He had been so strong and there had been something so secure and reliable about him that it had swept away all fear and these last weeks had been golden days of sheer, undiluted happiness.

'Suppose I ... never know them ... again?'

She almost felt the question being asked out loud; and then as she wanted to cry out at the agony of thinking she might have lost him forever, she knew that she loved him!

She loved him in a manner in which she had never envisaged it possible to care for anyone.

It was the giving not just of her heart but of her whole and complete self.

She loved him, she realised, with every thought she had, with every breath she drew, and yet she had not been aware of it.

'How stupid ... how foolish I have been!' she told herself.

She might have known it was love when she had found herself happy only when she was with him and it had been hard to go to bed because she must leave him and so many hours must pass before she would see him again.

She might have known it was love when she awoke in the morning with a feeling that something wonderful and perfect was going to happen.

But she had never analysed to herself why she was looking forward so eagerly and excitedly to seeing the Duke.

"I love him! I love him!" she said now.

She knew now that the pain in her breast when he had left her to go to the beautiful Lady Moreton had been jealousy.

Jealousy because she was afraid of losing him, and jealousy because this other woman was so much more lovely than she could ever hope to be.

'Oh, God, let him love me a . . . little,' she prayed, 'just for a little while.'

She knew that if ever she had to leave him she would want to die.

She thought now of how much time she had wasted in not being aware of her love, of not showing him how much she cared and how much it meant to her to be beside him.

Then she told herself that it would have made no difference to him, and what he felt for her was kindness . . . the kindness of a man who has befriended someone in trouble.

But he obviously had no other feelings for her.

For the first time she wondered how she could have stayed alone in the Villa with the Duke without thinking it wrong or at least shockingly unconventional.

It had seemed so unquestionably right that it was only now that she realised what interpretation the outside world might put upon it.

Perhaps, she thought in sudden horror, Lady Moreton had said scathing things about her after finding her in the Sitting-Room; perhaps she had repeated to her friends, and would certainly repeat to other people in England or in Monte Carlo, that the Duke had not been alone.

'They will assume that I am his mistress,' Salena thought, remembering that that was what the Prince had intended to make her.

Yet, instead of being shocked or in the least horrified, it struck her that to be with the Duke and to be loved by him would be the most perfectly wonderful thing that could possibly happen to her.

What did it matter what names she was called or what the world said?

If he wanted her, even for a very short time, she would die happy, knowing she had tasted the fruits of Paradise and nothing else in life could ever be the same.

"Love me . . . love me just a . . . little,' she called to him.

She wished that she could have told him how much he meant to her and how, in the language of the country they were in, she was "at his feet."

"That is where I am and where I want to be," she said.

Then once again she cried out to him desperately to come to her so that she could tell him of her love.

The camel was travelling fast again, and as she was rocked backwards and forwards in the howdah, Salena wondered if she would become sick from the movement.

She thought, in fact, that she was more likely to suffocate, for she was very hot and the dark cloth which had been pulled so tightly round her seemed to press against her face almost as if it were a mask.

They seemed now to be moving almost silently, and she was sure that now the camels were walking on sand.

The idea of being carried away to one of the desert plateaux was frightening because these were the places occupied by the fierce Berbers.

She remembered that the Duke had described with a laugh quoting from some poem she did not recognise as:

> A fair and whited sepulchre
> full of dead men's bones.

The memory made Salena shiver.

Perhaps that was what would happen to her: her bones would be left in the sand, and the sun would whiten them until no-one would ever be able to tell to whom they had once belonged.

By now they must have travelled for well over an hour, perhaps longer.

Suddenly, when she felt almost mesmerised by the rocking motion of the howdah, there was a word of command and the animal on which she was riding came to a standstill.

With grunts and groans the camel went down on its front knees, and then as Salena fell forward the animal lowered its back legs and the howdah righted itself again.

She felt hands undoing the ropes which tied her to the howdah on which she had been sitting, before being picked up bodily by two men who carried her away from the grunting camel.

Now she knew for sure that they were in the desert; there was no sound of footsteps, and the men seemed to move smoothly, almost as if their bare feet slid deep into a stoneless surface.

They walked for a little distance. Then a man spoke to them, and Salena had the idea because they lowered her a little in their arms that they bowed their heads at an entrance.

Her feet were then on the ground and the rope was being untwined from her body.

She drew in her breath and knew that now the moment had come when she would see her captors.

She was afraid of the faces she might see—evil, menacing, and cruel. They would be the faces of men who were prepared to risk the death penalty to obtain the money they needed.

The ropes that had tied her ankles and her body fell to the ground, and then the cloth that covered her was lifted.

It was swept back from her head and for a moment it was impossible for Salena to see where she was, because her eyes were dazed from the darkness of the confining cloth and the place to which they had brought her seemed dim.

Then she realised she was in a tent, a large tent draped with rugs and furnished with low, cushioned seats, Eastern fashion.

She was standing in the centre of it, and because her hair had been pushed over her face by the cloth she put up her hands to sweep it back, aware as she did so how hot she was from being confined.

Only then did her sight seem to clear, and she saw that at the far end of the tent, lounging on a low couch and watching her, was the Prince!

For a moment she thought she was dreaming. Slowly he raised himself to a sitting position.

As she stared at him incredulously, too astounded to utter a sound, he smiled, and it was not a pleasant sight.

"You are . . . not dead!"

The words seemed to burst from her.

"No, I am not dead," he answered. "And I might have said the same words to you, if I had not learnt two days ago that you were alive and enjoying the society of a nobleman!"

There was something very unpleasant in the way he spoke, but Salena could think of nothing but the fact that he was there and she had not killed him as she had thought! Terrifyingly, she was once again in his power.

Instinctively she looked for the two men who had carried her, but they had vanished. She was alone with the Prince.

140

As if he knew what she was thinking, he said:

"I have made sure this time that there are no weapons with which you can attack me and no method by which you can escape."

"I did not ... mean to ... kill you," Salena said in a low voice, "but when I thought it had ... happened and you were ... dead, I tried to ... drown myself."

"That was what I believed had occurred," the Prince replied. "A servant saw you running across the garden, and when you did not return, everybody assumed that you had drowned."

"I was ... picked up by ... a ... yacht."

"So I have learnt. How very convenient that it was such a luxurious one and your rescuer was the noble, and of course attractive, Duke of Templecombe!"

"How did you know that?" Salena asked in surprise.

"My informant was a lovely lady to whom the Duke belongs."

Now Salena understood.

Lady Moreton had come to Tangier in the Prince's yacht. Having called on the Duke and seen Salena, she had told the Prince that she was with him.

It was not difficult for the Prince to guess how it had come about.

"Lady Moreton described you very accurately," the Prince said. "And I knew that it was only right that I should claim what I had paid for and what belongs to me."

There was something in the way he spoke which made Salena acutely aware of the manner in which he threatened her, and she looked round once again for a means of escape.

"Before you bother to try the exit," the Prince said, "let me inform you that my servants have instructions to stop you from leaving the tent and also to bring you back immediately should you escape and run away into the desert."

"I will not ... stay here with ... you!" Salena cried.

"You have no choice," the Prince answered, "and besides, I assure you we shall be quite comfortable. The Sultan has lent me, or rather hired, this very luxurious tent and the servants to man it, and he has even provided me with a woman to wait on you."

"I will not ... stay!" Salena repeated. "You ... deceived me with a fake marriage, and I owe you nothing ... not even ... gratitude!"

"I bought and paid for you," the Prince answered, "and I do not allow myself to be tricked, least of all by a woman who is as attractive as you."

His eyes flickered over her and once again she felt as if he were undressing her and she was standing naked before him.

Because she felt despairingly that he was speaking the truth when he said there was no way of escape, she moved a little towards him, then flung herself down on her knees.

"Please let me ... go!" she pleaded. "You must realise that I hate you and have no wish to be your ... mistress. There must be many ... women who would be ... grateful for what you can ... give them and who would ... love you in return."

The Prince smiled again, and it made his face seem even more evil than before.

"I like to see you on your knees, Salena," he said, "and that is where you should be, after the manner in which you treated me. You have not enquired yet after my health."

"I told you that I did not ... mean to hurt you—certainly not to ... kill you. It ... it just ... happened."

"Most unfortunately," the Prince said. "But there are skilled Doctors in Monte Carlo who patched me up so that I am still capable of making you mine, as I intend to do."

"No!"

Salena rose to her feet.

There had been something so menacing in the way the Prince spoke that it was no longer possible for her to think clearly. She ran across the tent in the direction from which she knew she had entered it.

She pulled aside the curtain which covered the opening.

Outside were standing two turbaned servants wearing huge, loose white pantaloons and red sleeveless boleros.

They were tall, dark-skinned men with clear-cut features, which told her that they were Berbers, and she thought there was something ferocious and threatening in the manner in which they regarded her.

With a sound that was almost a cry she let the curtain fall, and as she did so she heard the Prince laugh.

"You see, my little dove, there is no escape," he said, "so let us enjoy ourselves. What can be more conducive to romance than the vast emptiness of the desert and a man who will teach you about love?"

"What you are offering me is not love," Salena said passionately. "It is wrong and wicked. Let me go and I promise that somehow I will pay you back the money you gave my father."

She saw by the Prince's expression that he was only amused by her pleas, and her voice strengthened as she said:

"If you keep me here, I swear I will try to kill you."

"With what?" the Prince asked.

He made a gesture with his hands which indicated that the room was empty of everything but the soft-cushioned seats, the low brass coffee-table, and the beautiful rugs which covered the floor.

Salena clenched her hands together, knowing he was mocking her, knowing he enjoyed in some perverted way of his own the fact that she was afraid and was trying to escape.

"You see, my little dove," the Prince said in the silky tones she had always disliked, "the cage is well

143

contrived. Now, as I know you must be hot and perhaps tired after your journey, I will allow you to bathe
and change. Then we will talk again. I have a great
deal to say to you."

He clapped his hands, and from the other side
of the tent, behind where he was sitting, the
curtain was raised and Salena saw a native woman.

Because to escape from the Prince's presence
even for a few moments was in itself a relief, she
walked towards the woman but before she reached
her the Prince said with an amused note in his voice:

"Just in case you should contemplate trying to
bribe her, she is a deaf-mute. Very useful, the Sultan
assures me, in certain circumstances."

"A deaf-mute!"

As Salena repeated the words to herself she felt
as if they made the prison to which she had been
brought more frightening and more unpleasant than
it was already.

Because there was nothing else she could do,
she passed through the curtain which the woman held open for her.

She found herself in what appeared to be a small
tent which was attached to the huge one in which the
Prince was sitting.

It was, she was sure, the type of tent used by Sul-
tans and important Arab leaders when they travelled
about the country with a huge caravan.

It would be carried on the backs of animals and
erected in an oasis or anywhere they wished to stay.

The larger the tent and the more luxurious from
the Moroccan point of view, its furnishings, the more
impressive was its occupant.

The tent in which she found herself had the
floor covered with exquisitely woven carpets and
there was a couch piled with silk cushions and what
to Salena seemed for the moment a joy she had not
expected, a tin bath filled with jasmine-scented
water.

She was so hot from being covered and bound and rocked about on the camel's back that she allowed the deaf and dumb woman to undress her, noting that she was obviously experienced at her job.

In the cool water Salena tried desperately to think of how she could escape.

She was sure that the Prince had a number of servants with him, either his own or ones borrowed from the Sultan, and he had not been speaking idly when he said they had been told not to let her get away.

Besides, having been unable to see the way they had travelled, she had no idea in which direction Tangier lay, or indeed if there was anywhere she could hide even if she could escape from the tent.

'I have to plan! I have to find some way!'

Once again her mind went to the Duke, and she began praying that he would come to her. But how he could do so she had no idea.

The woman brought her a towel with which to dry herself, but when she looked for her clothes she could not see them.

In sign language she told the woman what she wanted, and in answer the woman picked up from the couch what had appeared to Salena to be a number of gauze scarves.

As she looked at them she saw in horror that it was in fact a native costume.

For a moment she could hardly credit that this was what the Prince intended.

Then she knew it would be just like him to provide her with something sensuous and exotic and to deliberately prevent her from putting on her own clothes.

That indeed was what he had done, and although she tried to explain in every way she could that she wanted the gown in which she had arrived, the native woman merely pointed with quiet obstinacy to the garment on the bed.

145

Salena told herself that she was faced with the alternative of going in to the Prince clad only in a towel, or of putting on the dress he had provided.

Gritting her teeth, knowing there was no other course open, she allowed the native woman to drape her in the soft, diaphanous veils, for they were little more, in which the Moslem women dressed in a Harem.

They veiled her body and yet there was something so seductive about the effect of the light, soft-coloured *mansouriah* that she knew with a shudder it was what the Prince intended.

There were embroidered *babouches*—soft slippers—for her feet, and two elaborate necklaces, ear-rings, bracelets, and a head-band with hanging pearls.

When she was dressed, the woman brought from a corner of the tent a mirror so that she could admire herself, but all Salena could see were her eyes, dark with fright, and her mouth, which was trembling.

"What can I do?" she asked her reflection. "What can I do?"

There was no reply.

With a courage she was far from feeling and an agony of fear that seemed to run through her from her head to her toes, she passed through the curtain, which the woman held to one side for her, and entered the tent where she knew the Prince was waiting.

He was reclining on the couch on which she had first seen him, dressed in Moroccan fashion in a *serwal*—trousers which were very loose round his hips, with tapering legs that hugged his calves.

He wore an open-necked shirt which made him look as old and heavy as he had seemed in Monte Carlo.

In front of him was a low table covered with the sweetmeats with which the Moroccans invariably began and ended their meals.

She saw that he was sipping wine, which she knew was against the Moslem religion, and she thought contemptuously that he made his own rules and would certainly pay no attention to the beliefs of his friend the Sultan.

"Come along, my pretty dove," the Prince said to Salena. "I have been waiting for you with ever-growing impatience. Now let me see how you look in the very delectable clothes I have chosen for you."

"You had no right to take away my gown!" Salena replied.

She thought that instead of conveying her anger her voice sounded weak and helpless, and she felt that already she was becoming the submissive woman the Prince wanted her to be.

"Let me give you a glass of wine," he said.

He made a gesture with his hand and a servant who was standing at his side filled Salena's glass as she sat down on a cushion facing the Prince, with the table between them.

"Now I can admire you," the Prince said. "You are still the most beautiful and desirable woman I have ever seen! How could you imagine for one moment that I would forget you?"

Salena did not answer.

Because she felt weak and limp she drank a little of the wine and accepted the food that was offered to her.

"This is what I have planned, what I have looked forward to," the Prince said.

"Do you imagine that the Duke will let me disappear in this mysterious way without making enquiries?" Salena asked.

She felt the wine giving her a little courage and she spoke loudly and positively because it was a contrast to the soft, insidious, and caressing tone used by the Prince.

"I think you over-rate your attractions," the Prince replied. "As I have already told you, he belongs to Imogen Moreton, and in her arms he will soon forget the waif he fished out of the sea."

If he had struck her with a dagger he could not have hurt Salena more.

She was sure that Lady Moreton would have contrived all too willingly to keep the Duke amused while Salena was abducted from the Villa.

Now she would tell him not only who her father was, but how much the Prince wanted her and that he need no longer feel it incumbent upon himself to rescue her.

For a moment the agonising thought of the Duke and Lady Moreton together made her oblivious to her own peril.

Then she remembered that she had told the Duke very positively how much she hated the man who had tricked her into a fake marriage and how terrified she was of him.

'He knew I was speaking the ... truth,' she told herself. 'He will know how ... frightened I must now be.'

Once again her whole being was crying out to him to save her.

As if the Prince read in the expression on her face what she was thinking, he said:

"I shall not allow you to be unfaithful to me even in your thoughts. You belong to me, Salena, and the sooner you accept that, the better! You are mine and after tonight there will be no escape. I doubt if even the Duke will be interested in you once your body belongs to me."

"I will ... die first!" Salena said.

"Do I have to beat you into submission as I did before?" the Prince asked.

Now there was a cruel, sadistic look on his face, which made Salena shrink back as if he had put out his arms towards her, although he had not moved.

He saw how afraid she was, and he laughed.

"You must learn to do as you are told, my fluttering bird," he said. "You must learn to be submissive. You must learn above all things to be a woman as God intended you to be."

His words seemed to sear her, as if he were already wielding the whip she feared.

There was no point in arguing, no point in defying him, she told herself. All she had to do was find some way to die before he did what he intended. There would be no other way of stopping him.

The servants brought them food. The *harera* was a soup of mutton, chicken-livers, chick-peas, and a dozen other ingredients. Salena knew that it was believed to restore strength, and it frightened her to guess why the Prince had chosen it.

After this came *bstila*, the zenith of Moroccan gastronomy, containing the meat of pigeons with eggs, spices, cinnamon, and one hundred and four layers of pastry.

There were other dishes, which the Prince and Salena ate in Eastern fashion, with their fingers, and she was well aware why he had so arranged it.

It was quite a long meal. However badly she had wounded him, Salena saw that it had not inhibited the Prince's appetite.

He also drank a great deal of the wine, and the more he drank the more his eyes seemed to flare with the passion she knew he felt for her.

It made her feel that he was a wild animal waiting to spring on her and devour her.

She ate only a few mouthfuls of each dish, forcing herself to swallow simply because she felt it might give her the strength to resist the Prince, although she had no idea how she could do so.

The meal was finished and the servants carried away not only the plates and glasses but also the table at which they had eaten.

Now there was nothing between Salena and the Prince but a few feet of carpet.

"Come here!"

It was a command, and now she knew that this was the moment when she could no longer fight him and instead must take her own life.

She had no idea how she could do so. Since she

could swim, she had been unable to drown herself, and she was certain it would be very hard, if not impossible, to prevent herself from breathing.

She felt that the trap into which she had fallen was closing in, the walls of the tent were growing closer, and the Prince's eyes appeared to grow larger.

He was hypnotising her, she thought wildly, and with an effort which seemed to jerk her whole body Salena looked away from him.

She wanted to speak, wanted to plead with him once again, but her lips were dry and the words would not come.

"I gave you an order," he said softly and insidiously. "Come here, Salena!"

It was impossible for her to move; she felt as if she were nailed to the couch on which she sat.

The Prince raised himself.

"Do I have to make you obey me?" he asked.

Now there was a note in his voice which told Salena that he was excited by her defiance.

She stood up. As she did so, she saw that he held a whip in his hand, and she screamed. . . .

* * *

The Duke walked through the corridors which led to a small Sitting-Room by the front door, where, he had told the servants, anyone who called in the future was to be kept waiting.

He entered the room to find Imogen, as he had expected, looking extremely beautiful, bedecked in an alluring gown that he suspected had been chosen deliberately for his benefit.

"You wanted to see me?" he asked, and his tone was uncompromising.

"Yes, Hugo. I had to see you. It is most important."

"What is?" the Duke enquired.

"When I collected my jewels from the *Aphrodite* I found that some were missing."

"That is impossible!" the Duke replied. "They were in Dalton's keeping and you know that not only would he not touch anything himself, but he would certainly prevent anyone else from doing so."

"Well, I cannot find the emerald ring you gave me, and you know, dearest Hugo, how much I treasure it."

"You had better look again."

"You gave it to me," Imogen went on in a reminiscent voice, "the night after we first made love together. Darling Hugo, how wonderful it was, and how happy we both were!"

"I have already thanked you for the happiness you gave me," the Duke said coldly, "and I really think, Imogen, it is slightly embarrassing and quite unnecessary for us to discuss the intimate details of the past."

"But I want to do so," Imogen replied. "I want to remember everything you said to me and everything we did."

She gave a deep sigh.

"You taught me to love you so desperately, and there will never—I repeat, *never*—be another man in my life."

The Duke smiled cynically.

"You can hardly expect me to believe that, Imogen. I have asked no questions, but I cannot believe that you have journeyed to Tangier alone in a steamer with a number of tourists."

"No. I came with Prince Serge Petrovsky," Imogen replied.

She saw the expression on the Duke's face and said quickly:

"There is nothing like that about it. He was ill. Some woman had stabbed him, and even if he had wished to be my lover it would have been impossible."

Suddenly the Duke was still.

"You say some woman stabbed him?" he asked.

"Some girl with whom he was infatuated," Lady

151

Moreton said quickly, as if she thought she had said too much. "But I am here to talk about us, not about him."

"All the same, I am interested," the Duke replied. "Who was this girl and what was her name?"

"I cannot remember," Lady Moreton answered evasively. "What I want to talk to you about, Hugo, is my emerald ring. Please—you must help me find it. Let us go to your yacht now and see if it could have been left behind."

"If it is there, Dalton will find it," the Duke answered. "But I cannot help feeling, Imogen, that even if it is lost it is not the real reason for your coming to see me."

Imogen Moreton opened her blue eyes very wide.

"Why should you imagine . . . " she began. Then she changed what she had been about to say.

"Of course I wanted to see you," she continued. "I would have made any excuse if only we could be happy together as we were before you left Monte Carlo."

The Duke did not reply and she went on:

"Surely you are not still angry with me because Boris kissed me? Oh, my dearest Hugo, you must grow up and realise that you and I are sophisticated people."

"I have no wish to discuss it, Imogen," the Duke said wearily. "Go back to your Prince and tell him—"

He was interrupted as the door opened and Mr. Warren came hurrying into the room.

"Forgive me, Your Grace," he said, "but I have something of the utmost urgency to convey to you."

The Duke looked at Imogen and she sat down in a chair.

"I will wait," she said sweetly. "I am really in no hurry."

The Duke hesitated, as if he would command her to go, but then he went from the room, followed by Mr. Warren.

"What is it?" he asked.

"It is Miss Salena, Your Grace."

"What about her?"

"I am afraid, Your Grace, that she has been abducted!"

The Duke stared at the elderly man incredulously.

"One of the gardeners tells me he saw her being carried away by four men. They threw a cloth over her and carried her from the garden. He was too frightened to try to stop them, but came at once in search of me."

"How long ago did this happen?" The Duke's voice was sharp.

"Perhaps ten minutes ago, or a quarter of an hour, Your Grace. I was not in my house but in the stables, and it took the man some time to find me."

The Duke did not speak and after a moment Mr. Warren said:

"I am afraid it may be a question of a ransom, Your Grace."

"I think not, Mr. Warren."

The Duke stood for a moment, thinking, while Mr. Warren waited, then he said:

"Send a carriage to the yacht with all possible speed and bring back the Captain and every man who can ride. Tell Captain Barnett they are to bring rifles with them."

Mr. Warren looked surprised, but he had been too long in the Duke's service to question any order he was given.

"Have every horse in the stables saddled," the Duke continued.

Without waiting for Mr. Warren's reply, he turned and went back to the room where he had left Imogen.

She was smiling as he shut the door behind him, and as he walked towards her she asked:

"What has happened? Why are you looking like that, Hugo?"

"I want the truth and I want it quickly!" he said. "You told Petrovsky about the girl who is staying here?"

"What if I did?" Imogen countered. "There is nothing wrong in that."

"He told you, then, that she was the girl who had stabbed him and who he thought had drowned."

The Duke snapped the words at her and he thought for a moment she was going to deny it, but then with a shrug of her shoulders she said:

"What if he did? I do not concern myself with your flirtations any more than you need concern yourself with mine."

"Where has Petrovsky taken her?"

The Duke's question was almost like a pistol-shot.

"I have no idea what you are talking about," Imogen replied.

But he knew by the way her eyes flickered that she lied.

Chapter Seven

As the Prince came nearer and nearer, Salena knew that he was stalking her as if she were an animal he was hunting down.

She felt as if she could no longer move or think, but only cringe away from him against the folds of the tent.

She wanted to die. She wanted to collapse into unconsciousness so that she would not feel the agony of what was inevitable.

Then as the Prince reached her she saw the triumph and excitement on his face, and when he raised his arm she screamed again.

It was a very feeble scream, the cry of someone with no more strength to fight, someone utterly and completely defeated.

As she heard her voice, weak and ineffectual, there came suddenly the sound of other voices, and as a command rang out the Prince turned his head, surprised by the interruption.

The folds of the curtains parted and the Duke strode into the tent, followed by Captain Barnett and several English sailors with rifles in their hands.

For a moment neither Salena nor the Prince could move. He was still standing with his arm raised, a ludicrous expression of astonishment on his face.

But when Salena realised that the Duke really

was there she gave another cry—one of relief and inexpressible joy—as she ran towards him.

She flung herself against him, her arms went round his neck, and her lips were on his cheek kissing him with an abandonment that was purely instinctive and lacked all volition.

He put his arms round her and said quietly:

"It is all right, my darling. You are safe!"

Without looking at the Prince, he lifted her in his arms and started to carry her from the tent.

As he passed Captain Barnett he said:

"This gentleman is yours, Captain."

They passed two sailors who were holding the turbaned servants at gun-point, and Salena hid her face against the Duke's shoulder. She was trying to make herself realise that she no longer need be afraid.

She was safe, and he was holding her against his heart.

She felt him walking over sand and the air was cool on her cheeks, but she did not open her eyes until a minute or so later, when he came to a standstill.

Then she looked up at him and saw that waving over his head were the branches of palm trees.

"You are safe, my darling," the Duke said again. "He did not hurt you?"

It was a question, but Salena could only stammer incoherently:

"I ... p-prayed ... I prayed that you would ... come and s-save me."

"I thought that that was what you were doing," the Duke said in a deep voice.

He put her down on the ground but only so that he could clasp his other arm round her, and as she looked up at him wonderingly, his lips came down on hers.

Even as she felt the touch of him she knew it was what she had longed for, what she had prayed for, and what she had known would be a bliss and a rapture beyond words.

She pressed herself against him, feeling that she must become a part of him so that she would be safe forever.

Then as his mouth held her captive she felt as though something wonderful and beautiful and quite unlike anything she had ever felt before rose within her, moving up through her body, into her breasts, and then into her throat.

It was so perfect, so rapturous, that she felt she must in fact have died and reached Heaven itself.

At first her lips were very soft, sweet, and innocent, but as the Duke felt her quiver against him and knew that she responded to the insistence of his kiss, he held her closer still.

Salena forgot everything she had felt and feared. It had all vanished, while in its place the Duke gave her everything that was beautiful and perfect.

It was as if music enveloped them, and there was the fragrance of flowers, and they were no longer human but part of the Divine.

Only when at last the Duke raised his head to look down at Salena's face did he know that he had never before seen a woman look so radiant or so happy.

"I love ... you!" she murmured. "I love ... you!"

"That is what I have for a long time wanted you to say," the Duke answered. "But, my precious, I was desperately afraid that I would not be in time to save you from suffering at the hands of that unspeakable swine."

"He was ... going to ... beat me," Salena murmured.

Even as she spoke the words she felt they no longer had the power to terrify her. Because she was in the Duke's arms and he had kissed her, in some magical way her fears had disappeared.

"Let us go home, my sweet," the Duke said.

His lips found hers and once again he kissed her. He felt her tremble but it was not with fear.

He took one arm from her and turned her round.

157

She realised they were in an oasis, standing under tall palm trees, alone except for some camels a little way from them, lying down in the shade.

She looked back the way they had come and saw the tent, large and black, and outside it were a number of horses held by sailors wearing white uniforms.

She looked up again at the Duke.

It was impossible for her to think of anyone but him, and he saw with a relief he could not express that there was not the stricken terror in her eyes which he had feared.

Instead, her eyes seemed to have the light of the sun in them, and as if it reminded him that the day was drawing to a close, he glanced a little anxiously towards the west.

"We must hurry back," he said. "Are you strong enough, my darling, to ride? It would be quicker that way."

He smiled, and before she could answer he added:

"I promised we would ride together in the cool of the evening."

She gave a little laugh and put her cheek against his shoulder.

He picked her up again and carried her over the soft sand because it would have filled her light embroidered slippers.

As they reached the horses she saw that on one of them there was a side-saddle.

She waited for the Duke to lift her onto it, but he seemed to delay. She looked at him questioningly and saw that his eyes were on the diaphanous gown she wore, which revealed the curves of her breasts.

For the first time Salena thought of her appearance and felt shy.

The Duke gave an order to a sailor who had come from the tent, and the man turned and ran back.

"You look very lovely," the Duke said softly,

"but I have no wish for anyone but myself to see your beauty."

Salena blushed as the sailor came hurrying back with something in his hands.

"Will this do, Your Grace?"

The Duke took from him what he held and Salena saw that it was an exquisitely embroidered cloth such as in the East was thrown over couches, or, when ancient and valuable, hung on the walls.

The Duke put it round her shoulders, crossed it in front, and tied the ends at the back of her waist.

"Now you look a little more respectable," he said with a smile, and picking her up in his arms sat her on the horse's back.

She thought she must look very strange in her diaphanous Moorish dress with a band of hanging pearls round her forehead and glittering bracelets on her wrists.

But nothing seemed to be of any importance except that she was with the Duke and he had kissed her.

Captain Barnett came from the tent, followed by the sailors.

The Duke looked at him questioningly and the Captain said:

"His Highness will find it more comfortable, Your Grace, to lie on his face for the next few days!"

Salena had not listened or tried to understand what was being said. She had eyes only for the Duke, thinking how attractive he was and how much she loved him.

'He came to me when I called,' she thought. 'He saved me. He loves me as I prayed he would.'

The Duke swung himself into the saddle and they started off.

Salena knew that at first he set a slow pace, and when he realised how proficient a rider she was, they moved more quickly.

They soon left the desert behind, since, as Salena saw, the Prince had camped on the edge of it. Now they were moving through the foothills of the mountains until she saw the sea in the distance and knew it was only a downhill ride to the Villa.

By the time they reached the outskirts of Tangier, the sun had sunk and darkness was coming swiftly.

'We are home!' Salena thought.

But, to her surprise, the Duke did not go in the direction in which she knew the Villa lay, but headed towards the town.

They were riding too fast for her to ask any questions until after they made their way through the narrow, dirty streets, crowded with camels, donkeys, and beggars towards the harbour.

It was then that Salena realised they were making for the harbour and the *Aphrodite*.

With a sudden lilt in her heart she thought that they would not only be leaving the Prince behind but also Lady Moreton, and she would be alone with the Duke.

She knew she wanted more than anything else to be in his arms and for him to kiss her again.

Although it would be perfect wherever they were, it would be a wonder of wonders to know they were at sea and there could be no possibility of interruption.

The horses' hoofs clattered on the stone quay and they rode down the jetty to where the *Aphrodite* was gleaming white and elegant at the far end of it. In the lights from her port-holes, golden in welcome, Salena saw that Mr. Warren was waiting for them at the gang-plank.

The Duke dismounted then lifted Salena from the saddle of her horse.

She felt herself thrill because he was touching her. Her eyes met his and almost reluctantly he put her down on the ground. She walked towards the gang-plank.

"Everything is on board, Your Grace," Mr. Warren said.

"Thank you, Warren," the Duke replied. Holding out his hand, he added:

"Take care of everything until we come back."

"You may be sure of that, Your Grace."

With his arm round her, the Duke guided Salena onto the deck and then into the Saloon.

He shut the door behind him, and without thinking of anything but her need for him she turned to throw herself against him, her lips raised like a child's to his.

He looked down at her for a long moment before he said:

"I have something to ask you, my precious."

Because she wanted him to kiss her, she found it hard to listen to what he was saying.

"You are safe and you need not be afraid of ever seeing the Prince again," the Duke said, "but you will be safer still if you belong to me."

Now Salena looked at him questioningly. He smiled as he realised that she did not understand, and he explained:

"I am asking you to marry me, my lovely one, now—at once!"

He thought the expression of wonder that illuminated her face was like the dawn creeping up the sky, and then she made a little murmur and hid her face against him.

"I want ... more than ... anything else in the ... world to be your ... wife," she whispered, "but I ... I am not ... grand enough ... and I am afraid, too ... that you would find me ... boring."

The Duke held her very close and she felt him kiss her hair. Then he said:

"You are the most important person in the whole world to me, and I love you! I love you, my adorable one, as I have never loved anyone before."

Salena raised her head, and he added:

"That is true, and I shall prove it when you are my wife."

161

"Are you ... certain ... really certain?"

"Completely and absolutely certain!" the Duke interrupted. "And now, my darling, if you will wait here for just two or three minutes, I will make all the arrangements."

He kissed her gently, then before she could find anything to say he left the Saloon, shutting the door behind him.

Only when she was alone did Salena wonder what she looked like and if he could really think her lovely.

There was a mirror hanging on one wall of the Saloon and she moved quickly towards it to see her eyes glowing with happiness and her lips red from the Duke's kisses.

Her hair, thanks to the band which confined it, was not very untidy, but she pulled off the band because it reminded her of the Prince.

She pushed her hair into place, thinking that despite the place from which it came, the embroidered silk shawl which framed her shoulders was very attractive.

The necklaces glittered as she removed them, feeling that the Duke would not wish to see her wearing any jewellery that had been given to her by another man.

She flung the necklaces down on one of the chairs and unclasped the bracelets from her wrists. Then as the engines hummed beneath her feet and the ship began to move, she knew they were going out of the harbour.

She had escaped! The Duke had saved her at the very last minute, and he had said that he loved her! The knowledge seemed to fill the whole world and everything else faded into insignificance.

He loved her!

She had not imagined such a thing was possible, and yet her wildest dreams and yearnings had come true.

The door opened and the Duke stood there, and behind him was the Captain. The Duke crossed the Saloon to Salena's side and took her hand in his.

"It is entirely legal, my darling," he said, "for the Captain of a ship to marry his passengers at sea."

Salena gave him a radiant smile.

She knew why he was explaining to her that it was legal and that this would be no fake marriage such as the one with which the Prince had tried to trick her.

She had no words to say, and her fingers could only tighten on the Duke's.

He understood and for a moment as they looked into each other's eyes they were both very still.

Salena felt as if he was not only kissing her but that she was a part of him, and never again would she be alone or afraid.

* * *

The *Aphrodite* was still moving very slowly and Salena knew, because the Duke had told her so, that tonight she would barely make headway against the sea, so that there would be as little movement as possible.

She turned her head against the Duke's shoulder and although it was dark in the cabin she knew he was awake.

"I ... have been ... asleep," she said a little drowsily.

"You must have been very tired, my precious," he said. "You went through so much yesterday, and perhaps I was selfish to make you even more so."

She moved a little closer to him and put her lips against his bare skin.

"It was wonderful!" she whispered. "I did not know that ... love could be so ... marvellous ... so divine!"

"Did I make you happy?" the Duke asked.

"There are no words to ... express how I felt,"

Salena answered. "I love you and I want to keep saying over and over again that I love and adore you."

There was an unaccustomed little note of passion in her voice which moved the Duke deeply. Then he said quietly:

"That is what I prayed you would feel, my precious little love."

"I prayed that you would ... love me just a ... little," Salena said, "but you are so ... magnificent ... so clever ... so brave ... so everything a man should be, that I never thought my prayers would be heard."

"I do not love you a little," the Duke answered. "My love is boundless, as boundless as the sea and the sky."

Salena drew in her breath.

"Will you ... teach me so that I can ... keep your ... love?" she asked.

"I do not think you need be afraid of losing it," the Duke answered. "It is different, Salena, from anything I have ever known or felt before. When I first loved you, which was very soon after as a fugitive you came aboard the *Aphrodite,* I was afraid that you would always be fearful of men and of love."

"It was so foolish of me not to know that you were ... different and not to ... realise that when I was ... worshipping you at your feet it was ... love."

She paused, then said in a hesitating little voice:

"It was ... only when ... L-Lady ..."

The Duke put his fingers on her lips.

"Forget it," he said. "Forget everything that happened. Those people are of no importance to us and we are only concerned with the future."

Salena gave a little sigh and tried to move even closer to him as she said:

"You are ... right. We will not talk of ... them again, but there is ... one thing I must know, because I am ... curious."

"What is that?" the Duke asked.

"How did you know where to find me when I was carried away on the camel? I was afraid that once I was in the mountains it would be impossible for you to have any idea where I had been taken."

"That might have happened," the Duke admitted, "if I had not forced the information from someone who knew where you had been carried."

For a moment there was a grim note in his voice as he remembered how he had half-throttled Imogen to make her tell him where the Prince had gone.

He had also been fortunate that among his servants employed at the Villa was a man who at one time had been in the Sultan's service.

Because he no longer felt any loyalty towards an unjust master, he was prepared to guide the Duke and his party of sailors to where he knew the Sultan's tent was always erected on the first stop of any journey leaving Tangier.

Without such help, which seemed providential, the Duke knew that it would have been hard, if not impossible, to find Salena among the oases and the date-palms.

Because her happiness in being with him had swept away the terror she had experienced in finding herself once again in the Prince's clutches, he was determined that the past should be a closed book and they should concern themselves only with their future.

Aloud he said:

"Warren had all your clothes packed and brought on board, and, my darling, we will stop at various ports and buy you the things I have longed to give you but which you were always so reluctant to accept."

"I did not ... want you to be ... extravagant and ... spend money on me when I could never ... repay my debts."

The Duke laughed softly, remembering how she had protested at his buying her anything but the bare necessities when they had stopped at Gilbraltar.

In Tangier she had insisted on purchasing only the cheapest materials to be made up by native tailors.

He had understood that it was something to do with the Prince which made her afraid of being under an obligation, and he had not pressed her, but because she was so beautiful he wanted to frame her loveliness as it deserved.

"Now I can give you not only clothes," he said, "but jewels. We shall be able to buy some very magnificent pearls, and every other jewel, when we reach Constantinople."

"Is that where we are going?" Salena asked.

"It is known as 'the Pearl of the East,'" the Duke replied, "and I want to show it another 'pearl'—the 'Pearl of the West'—who is so precious and so beautiful that she really needs no adornment other than my kisses."

As he spoke he kissed Salena's forehead, then his lips moved over her arched little eye-brows.

It gave her a strange sensation which seemed to flood like sunlight from her heart into her throat.

Then as the Duke kissed her eyes one by one, then the tip of her small nose, her lips were ready for his, but instead he kissed her chin, her cheeks, and the corners of her mouth.

She felt the sunlight within her intensify until it was burning like the heat of the sun itself.

Her whole body seemed to quiver against his and she yearned for him in a way that she could not express.

Her need seemed to grow and grow until, before he could kiss her again, before his lips reached hers, she was kissing him.

She kissed him wildly and she knew as she felt his fiery response that this was what he had intended, and it thrilled her because she could excite him.

"I want you," the Duke said passionately. "I want you, my beautiful, adorable little fugitive from love."

His voice seemed to come from a long way away

and Salena felt as if everything were flooded with a celestial light.

It was a wonder which she knew was love but was so much greater, more glorious and more transcendent than she had ever imagined it could be.

"I ... want you ... too," she tried to say. "I want ... you and ... need you. I am yours ... completely and ... absolutely."

But she was unable to speak because the Duke held her lips captive and his hands were touching her body.

Then it was impossible to think, as there was only his lips, his hands, the beating of his heart, and him, in the whole universe.

ABOUT THE AUTHOR

BARBARA CARTLAND, the world's most famous romantic novelist, who is also an historian, playwright, lecturer, political speaker and television personality, has now written over 200 books. She has also had many historical works published and has written four autobiographies as well as the biographies of her mother and that of her brother Ronald Cartland, who was the first Member of Parliament to be killed in the last war. This book has a preface by Sir Winston Churchill. Barbara Cartland has sold 80 million books over the world, more than half of these in the U.S.A. She broke the world record in 1975 by writing twenty books, and her own record in 1976 with twenty-one. In private life, Barbara Cartland, who is a Dame of the Order of St. John of Jerusalem, has fought for better conditions and salaries for Midwives and Nurses. As President of the Royal College of Midwives (Hertfordshire Branch), she has been invested with the first Badge of Office ever given in Great Britain, which was subscribed to by the Midwives themselves. She has also championed the cause for old people and founded the first Romany Gypsy Camp in the world. Barbara Cartland is deeply interested in Vitamin Therapy and is President of the British National Association for Health.

Barbara Cartland

The world's bestselling author of romantic fiction. Her stories are always captivating tales of intrigue, adventure and love.

☐	2107	A VERY NAUGHTY ANGEL	—$1.25
☐	2140	CALL OF THE HEART	—$1.25
☐	2147	AS EAGLES FLY	—$1.25
☐	2148	THE TEARS OF LOVE	—$1.25
☐	2149	THE DEVIL IN LOVE	—$1.25
☐	2436	THE ELUSIVE EARL	—$1.25
☐	2972	A DREAM FROM THE NIGHT	—$1.25
☐	10977	PUNISHMENT OF A VIXEN	—$1.50
☐	6387	THE PENNILESS PEER	—$1.25
☐	6431	LESSONS IN LOVE	—$1.25
☐	6435	THE DARING DECEPTION	—$1.25
☐	8103	CASTLE OF FEAR	—$1.25
☐	8240	THE RUTHLESS RAKE	—$1.25
☐	8280	THE DANGEROUS DANDY	—$1.25
☐	8467	THE WICKED MARQUIS	—$1.25
☐	11101	THE OUTRAGEOUS LADY	—$1.50
☐	11168	A TOUCH OF LOVE	—$1.50
☐	11169	THE DRAGON AND THE PEARL	—$1.50

Buy them at your local bookseller or use this handy coupon:

Barbara Cartland

The world's bestselling author of romantic fiction. Her stories are always captivating tales of intrigue, adventure and love.